SOLDIER

ATTACK ON PEARL HARBOR

DOGS

READ ALL THE

SOLDIER DOGS

BOOKS!

SOLDIER
ATTACK ON PEARL HARBOR
DOGS

MARCUS SUTTER

ILLUSTRATIONS BY ANDIE TONG

HARPER FESTIVAL

An Imprint of HarperCollinsPublishers

To the crew of the *Arizona*, for their service and sacrifice.

HarperFestival is an imprint of HarperCollins Publishers.

Soldier Dogs #2: Attack on Pearl Harbor
Copyright © 2018 by HarperCollins Publishers
All rights reserved. Printed in the United States of America.
No part of this book may be used or reproduced in any manner whatsoever without
written permission except in the case of brief quotations embodied in critical articles
and reviews. For information address HarperCollins Children's Books, a division of
HarperCollins Publishers, 195 Broadway, New York, NY 10007.
www.harpercollinschildrens.com
Library of Congress Control Number: 2018947998
ISBN 978-0-06-288854-9 (trade bdg.) — ISBN 978-0-06-284405-7 (pbk.)
Typography by Celeste Knudsen
18 19 20 21 22   PC/LSCH   10 9 8 7 6 5 4 3 2 1
❖
First Edition

PROLOGUE

The attack came out of nowhere.

No warning, no declaration of war, no siren, before the enemy descended on the US naval base at Pearl Harbor in a wave of fire, panic, and destruction.

All across the island of Oahu, unsuspecting Americans were enjoying a perfect Hawaiian Sunday morning in what was as close to paradise on earth as one could get. Warm sunlight shone between the leaves of gently swaying palm trees. Stores and restaurants opened in preparation for a day of weekend shoppers. Hula music played softly on radios in windows and cars as coffee brewed and breakfast sizzled in pans. On the decks of the vessels of Battleship Row, a group of seven military battleships in port at the harbor, sailors were finishing up breakfast, playing a little early catch on deck, or getting ready for a weekend's shore leave with their wives and families.

Then, the roar of plane engines.

The crackle of machine gun fire. The thunder of bombs exploding. The thud of torpedoes slamming into ship hulls beneath the rocking waves.

America was being attacked.

That was all anyone knew.

On the deck of the USS *West Virginia*, Joseph Dean, eleven years old and son of the ship's head cook, had no idea the planes raining gunfire and destruction on him and his friends were from the Empire of Japan. He didn't know that the aircraft carriers from which those planes had taken off had left Japan eleven days earlier with plans to destroy Pearl Harbor. He didn't know the small black packages they dropped were armor-piercing bombs. And he had no way of knowing that the nearby USS *Arizona* had just taken on nearly 1.5 million gallons of fuel in preparation for a trip to the mainland.

All Joe knew was that Skipper, his new dog, had sensed something. She'd started barking at the edge of the ship, losing her cool in a way he'd never seen before. It had spooked them all—a warning of something they didn't understand.

A warning that came too late.

Joe watched as the planes appeared overhead. They swooped aggressively low over the ships along the row, bathing them in bullets and bombs. Suddenly Joe was dodging bullets and smelling smoke, and then—

BOOM!

A wall of white-hot air slammed into Joe. He flew through the air and landed on his back.

Joe sat up, dazed and hurt. Stunned, he could only watch as the *Arizona* was cut in half by a massive explosion. The ship's belly was like an opening into the pit from one of his grandmother's Bible stories, a raging fire that filled the sky with oily black smoke. As Joe tried to regain his bearings, the thirty-four-thousand-ton battleship began to sink to the bottom of the harbor after only ten minutes, the deafening blast taking with it over a thousand American lives.

As Joe stared on in horror, Skipper appeared in front of him. She barked and barked, trying to rouse him to action. Terrified and confused, Joe threw his arms around her neck and hugged her for dear life.

"Oh, Skipper," he cried, his body shaking against hers. "What's going on? Who's attacking us, girl? How did this happen?"

CHAPTER 1

SATURDAY, DECEMBER 6, 1941
5:30 P.M. HAWAII TIME

Joseph Dean glanced over his shoulder. The dog was still there, keeping a block's distance. He had to be following him, right?

Joe had first noticed the dog back by the docks, where he'd ridden his bike to search for shells. He was midway through digging up what he thought was a conch shell—it turned out to be only a piece of one, which was useless for his purposes—when he'd felt a prickle on the back of his neck. He was being watched. But by who?

He'd looked around the beach and didn't see

any people—and then he spotted the dog, watching him from the mouth of an alley between houses. Joe had kept digging for shells, acting like he didn't notice, but the whole time he'd felt the dog's eyes on him. Then, when he'd hopped on his bike and ridden away, the dog had appeared behind his bike, always a block away. Now it was obvious he was being followed.

At first, when the dog had come trotting out after him, Joe had been a little worried he was wild or rabid, especially given how dirty his paws and face were. But the dog's big, soulful eyes and the way his floppy ears perked up whenever Joe looked back at him made him look friendly.

I wonder if he's even a he, thought Joe absently. *Maybe it's a girl dog—*

He stopped himself right there. Why was he even thinking about it? Mama had enough mouths to feed with him, Pop, and Baby Kathy. She had enough on her mind. There was no way she was setting out an extra plate for some stray, even if that plate was just scraps.

Joe kept pedaling and tried to distract himself from the dog. He took a deep breath of the salty air and savored the evening around him. Even though the harbor was crowded with giant battle-ships and big industrial equipment, Pearl Harbor had one heck of a sky at sunset, calm blue giving way to blazing pink and burning orange at the water's edge. The warm breeze tasted like sea salt, the shells in his bike basket gave off a fishy smell that he kind of liked, and in the distance he could hear a seagull crying out. Even though he sometimes missed his family's old home in Texas, he had to admit that Oahu was pretty magical.

In a place this beautiful, you could close your eyes and forget that there was war brewing abroad—at least, until a B-52 from the American naval base ripped by and made your teeth rattle in your head.

Joe looked out into the sunset and did his best to keep his mind busy . . . but try as he might, he caught himself glancing back over his shoulder.

The dog was still there, looking friendly as ever.

Joe came to a halt, and the dog did the same. He smiled; it was like they both had the same feeling, wanting to get close but wondering if it was a good idea.

Darn it, why was he doing this? He'd have to get rid of the dog eventually. Better nip it in the bud while he had a chance.

"Go on, get!" said Joe, trying to sound mean.

The dog raised his eyebrows and looked over his shoulder before turning back to Joe. He looked like he was saying, *Me? Are you talking to me?*

"Get out of here!" said Joe, doing his version of Pop's hard voice, the voice he used when he had to work late or had taken guff from some loudmouth sailor who thought tormenting the mess hall staff was his patriotic duty. "You can't come home with me! Get going!"

The dog didn't move—but then Joe heard him laughing!

No, wait, that wasn't right. Whirling around, Joe locked in on the source of the laughter—two white sailors in blue uniforms, pointing at him while they shared a bag of roasted peanuts. They were young, barely out of high school by the looks of them, but swaggering like they thought they were commanding officers. He felt his cheeks burn as he lowered his head and tried to pretend he didn't notice them.

"Nice try, boy," said the sailor on the right, a short man with bright eyes and a sharp little smile. "Real tough guy, aren't you?"

Joe said nothing. Pop had warned him about sailors like this. They'd call you "boy" and tease you just so you'd react and say something mean; then they'd get you in trouble for talking back to a white man.

They're just bullies who like what little power they get by being born white, Joe told himself, repeating Pop's words. *The worst thing you can do is give them what they want. Then they win.*

"Say, kid," said the other sailor, a tall guy with a big block head, "why're you messing around with that dock stray anyway?"

"He just started following me home, sir," said Joe, laying the politeness on thick. Mama and Pop had always told him, even if a sailor is rude, you have to be polite back. Maybe they didn't deserve it, but it wasn't worth the trouble.

"Hey, Norman, isn't that the dog that's always swimming out by the *Tennessee*?" said the block-headed one, turning back to his beady-eyed friend.

"Oh *yeah*," said Norman, chewing peanuts

with his mouth open. "You're right, Mulvaney, it is! We've seen that mutt before. Swims over to some of the guys eating lunch, begs for scraps. You must be attracting him with your stinky basket of shells there."

The sailors walked over to Joe and peered into his bike basket. Norman sniffed, made a noise in his throat, and dropped his peanut shells into it.

That was it! Joe wheeled his bike back and picked the peanut scraps out of his basket. Before he could remind himself to be polite, he snapped, "This ain't a garbage can, jerk."

"Is that right? Sure smells like one," said Norman, his smile looking very mean all of a sudden. He took another roasted peanut from the bag, cracked it open, dumped the nut into his mouth, and flicked the shell at Joe's basket with a snicker.

"Whuff!"

All three of them started as the dog appeared between them. Joe hadn't noticed the dog closing in, but suddenly he was there, facing off against the sailors. The dog didn't growl or lower his head, but he let out one throaty bark—*Whuff*—that made Norman freeze in his tracks.

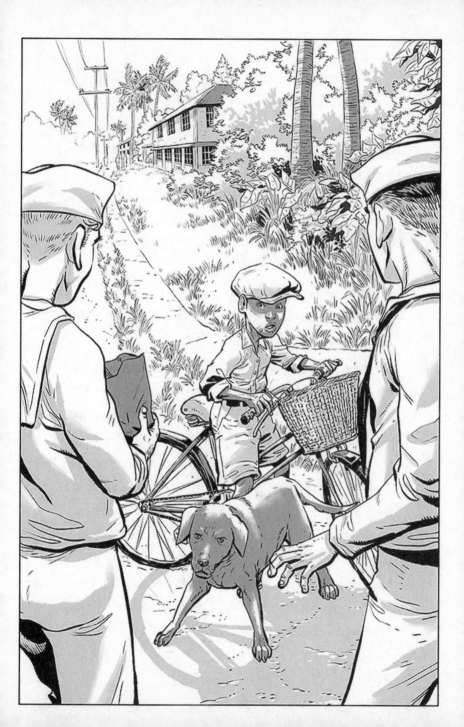

"Careful, Norman," said Mulvaney.

"Ah, it's fine, he's just a tough dog is all," said Norman. "Guess we know who the skipper of this ship is, huh, boy? Huh? I'm no trouble, boy. Who's a good boy? You want a peanut?"

"You're not supposed to give dogs peanuts," said Joe. "It's bad for them."

"Oh yeah, wise guy?" said Norman. "Says who?"

"Says my dad," said Joe. And just for good measure, he tossed in: "He's the cook on the *West Virginia*."

The name-drop worked—both men looked up at Joe with wide eyes.

"Your dad's Marcus Dean?" asked Norman.

"That's right," said Joe. He relished the glance the two sailors shared. Everyone respected Joe's dad, and not just for his Italian meat sauce. He was loyal, kind, and tough as nails. Besides, it was one thing to chew out a black serviceman on board a ship, but messing with his son on shore? Joe could tell these sailors knew better.

"Come on, Mulvaney, I'm getting bored," said Norman, shooting a glare at Joe. "Careful with that dog, *boy*. You can't be friends with every stray you meet by the docks."

"Thank you, *sir*," said Joe. As he watched the soldiers stroll off, he suddenly felt less sure of himself. Watching them run away at the mention of his dad was fun, but what if they were stationed on the *West Virginia* and saw Pop tonight for dinner? What if they mentioned him to Pop and complained that he'd mouthed off?

That'd be some birthday present for Pop, all right, getting chewed out by two angry white sailors coming back from shore leave.

Joe's worries were interrupted by a cold nose brushing his fingers. He looked down to see the dog nuzzling his hand with a big happy look on his face.

Joe couldn't stop himself—he pet the dog's face and gave him a scratch behind one ear. The dog's tail wagged like crazy.

Joe sighed. He knew Mama would be upset, and Pop probably wouldn't be all too happy either—but he couldn't just leave the dog out here. Especially not after he'd stood up for Joe!

"Okay," he said. "You can come with me. But

just for tonight, okay? And you have to be good. No barking or begging."

The dog sat and stared at him with wide, bright eyes. To Joseph, it looked as if he were standing at attention. He remembered the sailor's comment earlier, and he laughed.

"At ease, Skipper," he said. "Come on. Let's go home and I'll try to sneak you some dinner."

Joe got back on his bike and started pedaling. This time Skipper didn't keep any distance at all between them but ran alongside him with ears flapping in the night air.

Joe smiled down at his new companion. It was just for the night, he told himself, and the dog wouldn't cause any trouble. Anyway, what could happen in only a day?

Joe rode home with Skipper at his side, not knowing that in the next twenty-four hours, he'd be living in a country at war.

CHAPTER 2

Joe ate the last of his peas and stared daggers at the oven.

This was torture!

He didn't mind peas—heck, he even *liked* peas. But right now the whole house smelled like cake—the delicious almond cake that Mama was making for Pop's birthday tomorrow. And here he was, forced to sit at the kitchen table and eat chicken, peas, and grilled pineapple as though he couldn't smell cake baking.

Joe remembered from school that there was

an amendment in the Constitution that outlawed "cruel and unusual punishment." He wondered if Mama could get arrested for making him eat peas while the house smelled like cake.

Still, he wasn't so distracted that he forgot his plan. He pulled his napkin down on his lap, preparing for his next move. "Mama, can I have some more chicken, please?"

Mama looked up from where she sat with the baby by the radio. She went to the roasting pan in the kitchen and grabbed her tongs.

"Wing or breast?" she asked.

Joe remembered his grandmother giving chicken to her old Bassett hound Jesse back in Texas. She'd always pick out the bones, said dogs have a habit of choking on them. "Breast, please."

Mama grabbed him another chicken breast with the tongs and put it on his plate. From her arms, Baby Kathy gave him a little smile, like she somehow knew what he was planning. Joe winked at her, and the smile grew bigger. Good thing she couldn't talk!

The minute Mama turned away from him, Joe gave the piece of chicken a few jabs with his fork—no bones, perfect—and then moved it from his plate down to his napkin and pretended to be chewing a big mouthful. He wasn't sure if it would work, but as he watched Mama, he saw that distant look in her eyes, the one she got whenever someone on the radio talked about the war in Europe. She had too much on her own plate to worry about his.

"Everything okay, Mama?" he asked her.

"Hmm? Oh, it's fine, honey," she said, shaking her head as if she were trying to shake off the bad thoughts. She bounced the baby in her arms. "Just worried about the war, is all."

Joe felt his mouth draw down. The pineapple's aftertaste was suddenly very bitter. "The war" could mean anything. "Nothing's happened here, right?" he asked. "Pop's ship isn't going to the Pacific, is it?"

"No, thank God," she said. "Let's hope that doesn't happen any time soon. There's just more news from Europe. That Hitler's at it again, trying to invade Russia."

"How's he doing?" asked Joe, a little afraid of the answer.

★ 17 ★

"Apparently, his soldiers got caught in the snow and froze," said Mama.

"Way to go, idiot," said Joe.

"Joseph Dean, you watch your language at the dinner table!" she said. But underneath that reprimand was a laugh she couldn't help or hide. He smiled, feeling warm inside. These days, making Mama laugh was a victory. It was hard enough, what with everything going on in the world, but with a new baby and a husband who worked long hours on a battleship, she deserved every laugh she got.

Joe felt that warm feeling fade the more he thought about the war. The stories coming from abroad were totally crazy. He'd heard about Hitler, a twisted ruler in Germany who made dramatic speeches and expected people to worship him. Hitler was on the march across Europe now, taking over one country after another and rounding up Jews, black people, and anyone else who didn't fit his idea of the "master race."

Pop had told him about that, how Hitler thought there should be a ruling class of tall, blond, blue-eyed white people, and that anyone different than that should be rounded up and taken away by the government. In Hitler's eyes, Joe and his family were less than human because they were black.

Joe wondered what Hitler would say if he were standing in front of Pop, a hardworking man with a thousand-yard stare that made Joe stay out of trouble before he even thought of getting into it. Joe didn't think Hitler would give him a speech about how much better he was than Pop. Hitler would be like those white officers earlier today, shaking in his boots and walking away with his head down.

He felt the heat of the chicken through the napkin on his lap and remembered his next move. "May I be excused?" he asked.

"Of course," said Mama. "But clear and scrape first." Joe slipped the napkin in his pocket as he stood. He scraped his bones into the garbage, tossed the plate in the sink, and ran outside.

After hopping down his front steps, Joe scanned his narrow street. No sign of anyone coming out of the tiny houses.

Quietly, he headed to the alley between his

home and the Leesons' house and peeked behind the trash cans, next to his bike.

Instantly, Skipper hopped up and put his paws on Joe's shoulders. Joe tried to say "down," but instead got a face full of excited licks from the excited dog.

"Easy, easy." Joe laughed, pushing the dog back down. He brought the napkin out of his pocket, and Skipper began hopping and dancing so happily that Joe could hear his nails clicking on the ground.

When Joe unwrapped the napkin and revealed the chicken, Skipper froze in a half crouch, as though ready for the attack. Big gobs of drool rolled down Skipper's chop, and his head darted forward, but Joe said, "Hey! Wait!" and the dog froze, staring longingly at the chicken breast.

Joe lowered it to the ground, stepped back, and said, "Okay, now."

Skipper darted forward and wolfed the chicken breast down! Within seconds, it was gone.

"You're pretty smart, huh?" said Joe. He knelt down and let Skipper lick the last of the chicken grease off of his fingers. "I wish I could keep you. It would be nice to have a friend like you around."

Suddenly, Skipper raised his head, his ears perking up. He stared out of the alley, past the trash cans and into the street.

Joe felt the hair on his arms stand on end with this reaction. If Skipper was as smart as Joe thought, then he could tell someone was coming.

"What is it, boy?" he asked. "You smell something? Is there someone nearby?"

Skipper started barking loudly and jumped back into a crouched position.

"Hush! Be quiet!" he whispered, worried Mama would hear. He wondered who could be getting such a rise out of the dog—until he saw two faces coming around the side of the neighbors' house.

"Hey, guys!" he said, waving. "Over here."

"Joe?" asked Kai, wiping his sun-bleached hair away from his eyes and squinting into the alley. He and Millie walked tentatively toward him. "What are you doing in the alley?"

"The better question is, is that you barking?" Millie laughed. She walked with the beige navy-issue sack she used for collecting shells draped over her shoulder.

They peeked over the trash cans and saw Skipper at Joe's feet, and Millie gasped. "Oh my gosh, look at that beautiful doggy!" she said.

Skipper wasn't barking any longer, but Joe felt him standing stiff and ready at his side. "It's okay, boy, it's just my friends. Guys, this is Skipper. He followed me home."

"Why hello, Skipper," said Millie, kneeling down next to the dog and offering her hand. Skipper sniffed it and then gave it a nuzzle, and she rubbed his chin. "Yeah, that's a good girl. Hello."

"Wait, Skipper's a girl?" asked Joe. "How do you know that?"

Millie's mouth formed a small smile, and she rolled her eyes. "Her . . . *coat*," she said. "Labrador retrievers are always shaggier around the chest and shoulders when they're female."

"I didn't even know what kind of dog he, I mean, she was, honestly," said Joe, bumping fists with Kai.

"I think I know that dog," said Kai, smiling and giving Skipper an ear scratch. "She hangs around the docks, right?"

"That's what I've heard," said Joe. "Earlier today, a sailor told me that she swims for scraps down at the docks."

"Exactly," said Kai. "She gets a little jumpy when the planes buzz overhead, but she's a strong swimmer. And a strong smeller, by the sound of it. I'm impressed she smelled us that far away."

"Hey, speaking of smelling something all the way down the block," said Millie, nodding at Joe's bike, "how'd you do today?"

"Not bad," said Joe. He pulled the basket off of his bike and handed it to her.

He and Kai had met Millie while Kai was teaching Joe to surf over at Waikiki Beach. Joe and Kai had noticed Millie selling shell necklaces from a card table out by the Elks Lodge, and Joe and Kai decided to come over and say hello. They were talking to her when a couple of sailors came up to buy shell necklaces for their sweethearts— from Kai! Millie told them it was her first sale, even though her necklaces were really nice. Kai said they didn't just want a Hawaiian souvenir, they wanted an "experience," including buying their necklace from a native Hawaiian. Kai hammed it up—using Hawaiian words, pointing out the different kinds of shells on the necklaces, even referencing famous sailors and ships he knew from growing up in the area. Millie was sold out of necklaces by the end of the day. So they decided to go into business together: Joe collected shells, Millie cleaned them and made the necklaces, and Kai sold them down on the beach. They split the money three ways.

"Think these'll work?" asked Joe.

"These look great, actually," said Millie. "Thanks, Joe."

"And here's your cut," said Kai, handing Joe two faded bills. Joe's eyes bulged—two dollars! A fortune! He could buy his weight in candy. "You catch any waves while you were down there?"

"Nah," said Joe. "I was too busy looking for shells. Got hassled by a couple of sailors, though. *That* was fun."

"You should try being the one selling them," said Kai, rolling his eyes. "*Hey, hoa, do these shells have magical powers? Do you sell pineapple or coconuts too?* They think everyone here who's not a sailor is a professional tour guide."

"I bet— Hey!" They'd gotten distracted and hadn't noticed Skipper moving in. She had her head in Joe's bike basket and was tossing the shells around and sniffing for bits of fish.

"Cut it out, Skipper, these aren't for you," said Millie, trying to shoo her.

"Skipper, sit," said Joe.

Skipper stopped in midsniff, sat, and looked attentively at Joe.

"Whoa!" said Kai, laughing. "How'd you do that? Did you teach her that?"

"No," said Joe, surprised. "Skipper, lie down!"

Skipper lay down on the ground, paws folded in front of her.

"Shake?" said Joe, extending a hand.

Skipper sniffed Joe's hand and licked it.

"Two out of three ain't bad," said Millie. "She's one smart puppy. Are you going to keep her?"

"I don't think I can," said Joe, feeling down as he looked into Skipper's big, soulful eyes. "With the new baby, we already have too many mouths to feed, and Mama's worried about Pop onboard the *West Virginia*. I don't want to cause her any

trouble by having to care for a dog too."

"Does the *West Virginia* have a dog?" asked Kai.

"What do you mean?" asked Joe. "It's a battle-ship. They don't allow dogs on battleships."

"Sure they do!" said Kai. "I've seen a couple of ships with dogs here over the years. And my dad told me a story about a ship in England that has a dog named Judy on board, and how a couple of American ships are following their lead. The sailors keep them around as mascots, and it helps buck up the ones who have been at sea for a while. Do you think your dad could get her on board?"

At first Joe felt unsure—Pop was busy, and a dog might get him in trouble with sniffing around and getting up to no good. But then again, Skipper was a pretty good dog. She'd proven she was brave by standing up for Joe when those sailors hassled him, and she responded well to commands—she hadn't even eaten the chicken Joe brought her until he told her to.

And Skipper might make a lasting impres-sion on the other officers, which could only be good for Pop. He was always sore that the military still didn't consider black and white men equal, and he wished his higher-ups could see past his being black. ("Between you and me, some of them don't think much differently than that Hitler," he'd once told Joe.) Having a mascot might help him become a favorite around the ship and at least bridge the gap between him and the other sailors.

As Joe was thinking, a whiff from the kitchen hit his nose—the cake!

"Tomorrow *is* Pop's birthday," said Joe. "It could be a nice present." But then he imagined him offering Skipper to Pop and pictured the look on Pop's face at the idea of taking a dog to work. Joe frowned and shook his head. "But there's no way he'd bring her on board. He's too serious about his job. Tries to keep his head down, not cause trouble."

"Then we sneak her on board," said Millie. "Make it a surprise."

"How are we supposed to do that, genius?" asked Kai. "You have much experience stowing away on battleships?"

"I don't need it," said Millie. "I have a guy on the inside."

"Danny?" asked Joe.

"Danny," said Millie with a smile.

Millie began whispering her idea, and soon the three friends were hatching a plan.

CHAPTER 3

Skipper sniffed her coat and sighed again. All of her interesting smells were gone—the overflow from that hot dog stand Dumpster, the fish she'd rolled in under the dock, the dusty patch of road down by the park, all gone thanks to the boy-pup and his friends. They had sprayed her with a water tube, which had been fun at first when she was chasing the stream of water like it was a squirrel. But then they'd rubbed her down with a foul-smelling white bar, and she realized that they wanted to get rid of her smells.

The other dogs down under the docks would never let her live it down if they knew how smell-less she was.

Normally, she would have run away from the white bar and the water tube. But while the boy-pup Kai and the girl-pup Millie rubbed her down, the boy-pup Joe had put his hand on her neck and spoke to her, and it made her feel safe.

There was something about the way he looked at her and the way he spoke to her that made Skipper not want to run away. He had a good smell and a strong voice, and he said "sit" and "lie down" in a kind way.

Skipper snorted. She knew she should run away from Joe. The last master, the cruel and irresponsible Larry, had taught her that. He was so nice while Skipper had been a pup, and he had taught her the "sit" and the "lie down" and the "roll over." But then Skipper got bigger and wanted to play, and then Larry was mean. He had hit her on the nose with the rolled paper and left her outside when the sky poured water. Then one day he'd been very kind again, and he had taken her for a car ride and let her run on a beach.

She'd had a wonderful time chasing crabs and digging in the sand, but when she came back to the road, Larry was gone. She couldn't find him anywhere, no matter how much she barked for him. That was how she'd ended up living on the beaches.

Not that she minded much. The beach offered plenty of food and sun, and lots of water for swimming, which she loved. And there were always good smells by the dock, and the men in blue tossed her food when she showed them how strong a swimmer she was. But Skipper could always smell it before she saw it: the anger, the cruelty. She would shake the water off too close to a master in blue or grab some food off a seat, and she'd smell the anger taking over the human who'd just been nice to her.

And then? Then, "Get out! Go away!"

Then, newspapers and brooms! Kicks with hard boots! The men with the nets, closing in on her!

It was safer to run away.

But Joe smelled nice. True in his heart, like there was no anger in him. Like he would never say, "Go away!" He was the first human in a long time to look at Skipper like she was someone else, not just a fun thing for throwing food at. It made her not want to run away. She just had to be careful. You could never tell with humans.

Footsteps reached her ear, heavy and slow. Then, a smell—like Joe, but bigger, older, salty with sweat and bitter with burned food. Joe's master, she realized. Joe's alpha. Something else, too—something sweet and fresh. Flowers, like at the park.

Skipper crept to the mouth of the alley and peeked out.

There he was, much bigger than Joe but with Joe's eyes, his mouth at the corners, and that smell, trustworthy and strong. He wore a white shirt with marks of good smells on it, and he carried a bunch of flowers wrapped in paper in his hand.

Skipper watched Joe's father, making sure she stayed hidden in the shadows. As Joe's father got to the steps, the door opened and let out all the wonderful smells of the kitchen, and out came the woman. *Joe's mother*, thought Skipper.

Joe's father handed her the flowers, and she

smiled. He asked something about "Joe" and "Joseph," and the mother shook her head. Skipper knew Joe couldn't see anyone now; she could hear him only a few walls away from her, snoring and mumbling in his sleep.

Joe's father and mother went into the house, and with the closing of the door their voices and the kitchen's smells were quieted.

Skipper put down her head and closed her eyes. For the first time in a while, she didn't want to run at all. She wanted to be there for these people—to protect them and help them. Slowly, she sank into darkness, until she dreamed she was running on an endless beach chasing a giant crab with a soft shell and one broken leg . . .

CHAPTER 4

A hand touched her, and Skipper rose with a start and cried out, scared she'd been caught unawares by the men with nets.

But no, it was just the Joe pup. He put his finger to his lips and made the *shh* sound, and Skipper quieted down. It felt very early. Why was this pup up?

Joe waved to her, and she crept out of the alley into the street. It was morning now, pale and clear, so quiet and still that every smell and sound stood out.

"Skipper, come," said Joe. He climbed onto his wheel machine and pedaled off. Skipper followed alongside him, easily keeping pace.

While she ran, feeling the sleep blow away from her eyes, Skipper smelled the morning. It had to be *very* early, just before the sun came out. All around her were the smells and sounds of the town waking up—hot water pots bubbling, delicious-smelling garbage trucks rolling along, a loud bell in the distance, the repeating sound of water crashing onto sand . . .

And something else. Skipper's ears pricked up as she noticed the noise far off in the background, a buzz that she could barely recognize. It was a distant version of a noise she knew all too well, the call of the thing that made her want to run away more than any mean human . . .

Flying machines.

They were far off. They didn't sound like the ones she was used to.

And they were coming closer, very fast.

CHAPTER 5

"You keep quiet, okay, girl?" said Joe as he slowed down outside Millie's house in Pearl City. Skipper gave a little huff but stayed silent.

As Joe got off his bike and wheeled it silently up to the driveway, he felt his stomach knot and his blood pound in his ears. He'd been excited since he crept into the kitchen that morning and found fresh-cut flowers in a vase on the kitchen table. That meant Pop had been home.

Normally, Pop spent the night on the *West*

Virginia so he could rise early for breakfast. But this morning, when Joe had put his ear to his parents' bedroom door, he'd heard his father's signature snore. If he hustled, he could get Skipper on board the *West Virginia* before Pop was awake, without anyone noticing.

Millie's house was bigger and nicer than Joe's place, with carefully manicured bushes out front and colorful hibiscus flowers in the window boxes. A boxy dark-green army jeep sat in the driveway— Danny's car, Joe knew from Millie. The car that would help him sneak Skipper on board.

Joe crept up to the door carefully, hoping to get everything moving before a neighbor spotted him or Skipper barked.

He raised his fist to knock on the door—

And it quickly swung inward, making him jump back.

"Good, you're here," said Danny, Millie's older brother. He was gawky at eighteen, with skinny arms and legs wrapped in his blue naval uniform. His hair was mussed, and his eyes looked barely open and a little bloodshot, but at least he was here when Millie said he would be.

"Sure am," said Joe. "Thanks for doing this, Danny. It's really nice of you."

"Ah, don't worry about it," he said, hoisting a canvas rucksack over his shoulder and carefully closing the door behind him. "Where's the dog?"

"Over there," said Joe. "Skipper, come!"

Skipper broke her attentive seated position and bounded over to them. Danny got down and petted the side of her face while Skipper excitedly lapped at Joe's hand.

"Beautiful dog," said Danny. "Guess I have seen her around the docks. When Mills told me she was a dock stray, I pictured one of those scraggly island dogs that you see running around. But she looks real nice now that you guys cleaned her up and everything."

"You think the guys on the *West Virginia* will like her?" asked Joe.

"Oh, sure," said Danny. "A dog running around is good for the heart. And anyway, everyone loves a Labrador." He stood and nodded to the jeep. "All right, let's get going. The ship's going to be hopping soon. We want to get there while everyone's still too groggy to notice us."

They climbed onto the seats of the jeep, with Skipper sitting on the floor at Joe's feet. There were no doors and no top on the vehicle. When Danny started it up and it rumbled to life, Joe realized how easy it would be to fall out and gripped the edges of his seat tight. Danny didn't seem to notice, and Skipper popped her head out of the door and let the wind blow her ears back.

They took off toward the harbor, the loudest thing moving along the streets this early. As they drove through the quiet morning of Oahu, Danny said, "This is a sweet thing you're doing for your old man. Lord knows a dog could help buck up spirits on the old *Wee Vee*, and no one deserves to have their spirits lifted more than your dad."

"You know my pop?" asked Joe.

"Marcus? Yeah, sure," said Danny. "We've shot the breeze a couple of times. Funny guy. It's a shame, too, because he'd be a great soldier if the brass could just get their heads out of their keisters and realize that an American's an American, no matter what color he is."

Joe nodded, feeling bad for Pop. His dad

wanted to serve his country so badly, but black servicemen weren't allowed in combat roles in the navy. Mama quietly said under her breath that it was a blessing, that Pop should be happy enough at home with them. The last thing she wanted was him leaving their family and going to war. But Joe had seen the way it pained Pop to be a man with a soldier's bravery being unable to rise above third mess officer.

Up ahead, Pearl Harbor rose out of the horizon, a concentrated mass of squat buildings, giant battleships, and boxy control towers. Almost every surface had some sort of antenna on top of it or wire running from it, making the naval station look to Joe like a pile of military scrap with bits and pieces sticking out of it.

"Here we are," said Danny. "Keep that dog's head down."

A metal fence stood around the naval base, with the road leading up to a red-and-white-striped bar blocking their path. The jeep pulled up at a booth where a chubby old man with a baked-in tan gave them a lazy salute.

"Morning, Danny," he said. "How's life?"

"Ah, can't complain," said Danny. "Another day in the navy."

"I hear that." When the man saw Joe, he squinted. "And who's this with you?"

"This is Joe, Marcus Dean's boy," said Danny. "It's his birthday today, so Joe's going to surprise him onboard."

"Is that right, boy?" asked the older man.

Joe felt a sting, being called "boy" for the millionth time, but decided to let it go, and he focused on leaning forward to block the old man's view and keep Skipper out of sight.

"That's right, sir," he said.

The older man smiled and pressed a button. The bar lifted, and they drove into the docking area.

Joe felt a twinge of excitement as they entered the base. An actual naval base! Looking one way, he saw an airplane in a hangar, its engine being taken apart by an early-rising mechanic. Looking the other way, he saw boxes of ammunition: string after string of antiaircraft rounds, each bullet longer than his hand. All around him were the inner workings of a serious military operation. If only he had time to run around and see it all!

"This is so cool," Joe said softly.

"You think this is cool?" Danny laughed. "Don't forget those bad boys."

Danny pointed. Joe followed his finger—and looked out on Battleship Row.

The ships grew bigger and bigger in front of him, until they were looming ahead of them like man-made mountains. Their surfaces were a hodgepodge of iron railings and radar dishes that all led up to huge command towers at their middles. Joe counted seven overall, and he marveled at the bow of the ship they parked in front of, noting that some of the numbers stenciled on the hulls of the ships were probably taller than he was.

"Wow," he said, "they sure are huge."

"Definitely," said Danny. "The *Wee Vee* there is 624 feet long and weighs in at about 33,000 tons when it's full. That big ol' girl houses fourteen hundred sailors, so it better be big!"

"Fourteen hundred!" repeated Joe in awe.

"Oh yeah," said Danny. "Make no mistake, if Hitler gets one look at these babies, he's not even going to think about messing with us." He climbed out onto the dock and held up one finger to Joe. "Wait here, give me a second."

While Danny ran off to a small wooden shed, Joe reached down and petted Skipper. Something was up—she felt tense, and a shiver ran down her back. She kept looking back and forth from the battleship to Joe and back again. It worried Joe, so he tried to cheer her up with some scratches around the neck and chest.

"It'll be okay, girl," he said. "I know the ships are big and scary. But you'll like it here. Pop'll take good care of you."

Skipper gave a single bothered bark—"*HRFF.*" She looked up at Joe and then looked away.

Danny came walking back out with a big wooden crate in his arms. Inside was a bed of straw with an imprint in it that Joe recognized as that of a torpedo. He and Joe helped Skipper into the crate, and Joe got her to lie down in the imprint.

"We'll see you in a bit, Skipper," said Joe, his

heart twanging as he saw her sad face peering out at him.

"She'll be fine," said Danny, putting the lid back on over Skipper. "Come on, let's do this quickly. First breakfast is at oh-six-hundred. If we're lucky, we'll get to the kitchen right before your dad does." Joe got his hands under his side of the crate, and together he and Danny lifted and carried it toward the dock.

Danny led them to a metal platform that stretched from the dock to a large square opening right in the side of the *West Virginia*. The platform clanged and shook slightly under them as they made their way across it.

Joe glanced down and immediately realized he shouldn't have. The water, which always seemed a perfect blue to him at the beach, looked slate-gray and sudsy sloshing some forty feet under him. He snapped his head back up, looked straight forward, and tried to gulp down his fear.

He'd thought the *West Virginia* couldn't look any bigger than it had from the dock, but as they entered the loading door, the side of the ship turned into a gray wall of bolted-down metal panels. Between the ocean and the battleship, Joe felt like he was surrounded by giants that bore down on him with big gray faces . . .

But when they entered the ship, the whole world reversed—the passage they walked down was narrow and twisting, with pipes hanging overhead and handles coming off every wall.

The crate was hard to move in the passageways. Joe and Danny had to narrowly scoot through several sharp turns. As they came around one corner, Joe clocked his elbow against a ladder rung. "Yow!"

"Quiet!" hissed Danny. "Jeez Louise, kid, keep it down. We're not exactly *supposed* to be doing this, you know?"

The ship was full of distant voices and clanging metal. Joe worried they'd get caught before they got to the mess hall, but Danny seemed to know his way around pretty well. They entered the mess hall, a larger room with tables and benches that looked just as stark and industrial as the corridors that led to it.

Joe drank in the pipe-cluttered space with amazement and a little bit of sadness. He'd always pictured Pop serving food in a big hall with high ceilings. In here, Danny almost had to duck sometimes to avoid getting clocked with a pipe. No wonder Pop wanted to fly planes in Europe instead of spending his days cooped up in this giant tin can.

"Kitchen's back here," said Danny. They carried the crate into a wide room lined with metal countertops and stoves. They brought the crate to the back, where a small hall of lockers sat, and stopped in front of one with "MD" stenciled on the front.

"Okay," whispered Danny, and they lowered the crate. "So I'm thinking we put her in his locker and then wait around until your dad shows up. Then you say 'happy birthday,' open the locker, and—"

"Hey!"

Joe felt something like frost in his veins. He whirled around and looked into a pair of bright, familiar eyes. His stomach sank.

It was Seaman Norman, the sailor from down by the beach yesterday.

"Well, look who it is!" he cried. "Marcus's boy, come to visit his dad at work. What do you think of the kitchen, kiddo? Hope your dad likes working here, because it's as far up in the ranks as he'll ever get!"

Joe's face burned. He opened his mouth to reply, but Danny shot Joe a glance that said, *Don't bother.*

"I'm just showing the kid around, Norman," said Danny. "He wanted to surprise his dad. It's Marcus's birthday today."

"Is that right?" said Norman, nodding at the crate. "What's the deal with the torpedo crate? That a present for him, Cunningham?"

"Yeah, exactly," said Danny, exhaling hard. "We brought him a present, that's all."

"Mind if I take a peek?" asked Norman. He took a step toward the crate—

And the crate barked.

Joe jumped at the noise, its volume increased by their surroundings. The barking echoed along the walls, out of the kitchen and into the mess, along every rung and plate and ladder, bouncing through the metal maze of the *West Virginia*.

"What was that?" called a voice from the hallway. The sound of stomping boots got louder and louder.

CHAPTER 6

Joe shifted and sighed. The floor of the empty compartment was hard and cold. His butt was killing him.

He could almost feel the gaze of the officer who stood over him and Danny with his arms crossed. The man who'd been assigned to watch them couldn't be more than a few years older than Danny, but his square jaw, sloped brow, and insignia-covered uniform made him look like some troll who'd lived on this ship since the dawn of time. In the hour and a half they'd been locked in this room, Joe hadn't seen the guy move once.

All Joe could think about was Skipper, who whined and shivered across from him. He was officially worried. Skipper hadn't seemed scared coming to his place or getting in the jeep—what on the *West Virginia* was frightening her? He tried petting her, shushing her, scratching her belly, but nothing worked. She just couldn't be distracted from whatever was bugging her.

Finally, there was a loud clanking noise, and the door swung open. An older officer entered wearing a brown uniform and smoking a cigar.

"At ease, Sailor," said the old officer to the guard. The guard grunted and didn't move. The officer cocked an eyebrow and shrugged at them. Joe felt a little relieved—hopefully this guy wouldn't be all bad.

"Cunningham? Dean?" said the officer. "Let's go. On deck, on the double. Captain wants a word with you."

"Aw nuts," said Danny, climbing unsteadily to his feet.

Joe followed the older officer, Skipper at his side. As they walked down the hall, he noticed sailors peeking out of doors and hallways, laughing and calling out to Skipper, reaching out to pet her as they passed. Word must have gotten around that they'd brought a dog on board.

Joe felt like he might throw up. Pop probably knew. Meaning Pop had had to stand there and be filled in by a superior officer in front of his coworkers. Meaning when they got home, Joe was going to get a serious talking to. He might even get grounded. No more bike, no more beach trips, no more surfing . . . and most likely no more Skipper.

They followed the officer up a steep metal staircase and onto the deck. After being cooped up inside the *West Virginia* for so long, Joe had to put a hand over his face to shield his eyes from the early-morning sun. But as they adjusted, he saw the scene around him . . . and his breath caught in his throat.

The deck of the USS *West Virginia* was a vast expanse of gray metal, ready for war. Huge .50 caliber guns lined its deck, all leading up to two pairs of giant barrels jutting from the front. The towers stood overhead like skyscrapers, throwing shadows across them. All around them, sailors ran this way and that, loading gun magazines, checking knots, and mopping down the deck. On either side of the *West Virginia*, other huge battleships sat in the water, loaded with guns, towers, equipment, and sailors yelling at one another.

Joe spun and took it all in, his eyes widening as he saw the sheer size of the ship . . .

"Atteeen-*tion*," growled the old officer.

Joe turned back around and faced an officer in a white uniform covered with pins and badges, his lip bearing a thin, fashionable mustache. Beside Joe, Danny snapped up straight and saluted rigidly. At his feet, Skipper did the same, sitting stiffly with her head upright.

"Captain Bennion," said the older officer, "I present our smugglers . . . and their cargo."

Joe felt himself start to shake under the eyes of the highly decorated officer. His father had mentioned Captain Mervyn Bennion before, calling him a true American, a real son of the sea. Pop always talked about him with respect in his voice.

Well, thought Joe, *this is some way to meet him.*

Captain Bennion regarded them both, and then he looked to Danny. "Name and rank, Sailor."

"Seaman Apprentice Daniel Cunningham, sir," said Danny, a little quiver in his voice. "Construction and Engineering."

"Sneaking a minor and a stray dog on board a US battleship is a bad look, Cunningham," snapped Captain Bennion. "If you'd read the newspaper lately, you'd see that the US military has no time for tomfoolery. Too much is at stake. Understand?"

"Yes, sir," said Danny.

"And you, Mr. Dean," said Captain Bennion, looking down at Joe with just a hint of a smile. "Perhaps I should speak to your father about this when breakfast is over. Then he can decide your punishment."

"Oh no," said Joe, and without thinking he stepped forward and put his hand on the captain's arm. "Please, Captain Bennion, sir, please. It's his birthday, sir. I don't want him to spend it getting chewed out by his captain. He'll take my dog away."

Captain Bennion patted Joe's hand and nod-ded reassuringly. "All right, son. You just can't be bringing dogs on board behind a captain's back, even good dogs like . . . ?"

"Skipper, sir," said Joe.

Captain Bennion smiled wider. "A fine name for a dog." He crouched and reached a hand for Skipper's head.

All at once, Skipper went berserk! The dog began barking her head off and jumping around. Captain Bennion's hand shot back, and Joe felt struck with embarrassment—but then he heard her bark, really *heard* it. It was unlike any of her other barks: loud, full-throated, maybe even angry. He noticed the hair on her back standing up. Something was wrong.

"What is it, girl?" asked Joe.

Before any of them could stop her, Skipper ran to the edge of the carrier and began barking again . . . only it wasn't at the battleship across the water from them, it was in the air. She was defen-sively crouched, leaning back on her haunches, but barking straight up into the air.

Joe followed her gaze . . . and saw black shapes through the clouds in the distance.

"What do you make of that, Captain?" asked the older officer.

"Not sure, Harper." Bennion laughed. "I suppose she saw a seagull and it—"

"Look," cried Joe, pointing into the air.

All four of them went silent, watching the black shapes grow bigger . . . quickly. Slowly, a buzz could be heard over Skipper's barking. Around Joe, all the sailors on the deck of the *West Virginia* stopped in their tasks and looked up.

"Lieutenant Commander Harper," said Captain Bennion, "whose planes are those?"

"Not ours," said Harper. "Looks like . . ."

Just then, the black shapes swooped overhead, and tiny black packages dropped off of them. Joe only had a second to register them before they hit the deck of the battleship across from them and a deafening roar filled the sky.

The crew of the *West Virginia* cried out in terror. Blasts of orange fire and black smoke burst into the air from the deck of the other carrier.

Joe felt heat on his face and smelled burning rubber. He couldn't believe what he was seeing.

"Battle stations!" shouted Captain Bennion over the roar. "The *Arizona*'s been hit! We're under attack!"

CHAPTER 7

They were coming!

Skipper leaped wildly around as energy surged through her. She whimpered at the violent sounds now filling her ears and the smoke that was burning the inside of her sensitive nostrils. The masters had finally noticed, too, and they were running around trying to get ready for the enemy, but already the flying machines were raining fire on them.

She'd tried to warn them, but it was no use. The humans' ears and noses just weren't powerful enough. Now the flying machines were attacking, and the humans were hopelessly unprepared.

Skipper wasn't surprised—she'd always known the flying machines weren't their friends. Whenever they'd come roaring overhead or buzzing down near the docks, Skipper couldn't help but feel fear that drove her to hide under the dock or make her body small and low in the sand of the beach. The masters thought it was funny at the time, watching her get frightened, and they'd make their "aww" sounds whenever the flying machines passed overhead.

Well, they weren't laughing now.

All around her were running, screaming humans and more explosions, more bursts of smoke and fire, bits of grit and metal flying everywhere. The man in the shiny coat who had made Joe and Danny smell so scared was shouting orders.

Skipper tried to get her bearings, but it was nearly impossible. Between the flying machines, the fire, and the human chaos, she couldn't calm down! She wanted to fight back and stop the flying machines. She wanted to make it all stop.

Then, over the burning smell, she caught Joe's

scent and whirled, looking for him. She had to find him. Had to protect him. She didn't know why, it was just in her mind.

There!

Joe and Danny were crouched on the deck, Joe's eyes wide with disbelief. Skipper tried to run toward them, but there were too many humans in the way, too much noise and excitement. Every time she went for them, a new pair of legs hit her in the snout.

Skipper barked her emergency bark, hoping they'd hear her. *Get up!* she barked. *Get inside! Danny, get Joe home to his family!* It was no use. Her bark was swallowed by the noise, and Joe's attention was swallowed by fear.

Skipper darted this way and that, trying to find a break in the running humans. She needed to get to Joe. She wouldn't rest until she did.

That's when it hit her: this was why she was here. There had been something about Joe that she'd liked, something about his scent and his smile that had drawn her out of the alley. She'd told herself it was just the smell of the shells in his basket, but deep down she'd sensed something else. Now she understood it perfectly. She was always meant to protect him. He was her pup, her Joe.

Overhead, the flying machines buzzed low again, and other ships around them began lighting up with balls of fire and billows of smoke. Tiny bursts cracked, sending grit into to the air and knocking down some of the other humans. She needed to get Joe out of here, back on land and out of sight of the flying machines. She could hear other things in the sea besides the bubbling of water—strange beepings and whirrings, far off and powerful. She sensed other strange things approaching. If they were anything like the flying machines, then she had to get Joe out of their way.

There! A break in the running humans! Skipper darted toward Joe. She would get to him. Protect him, get him out of here, whatever it took—

KABOOM!

Noise ripped through Skipper's ears, and everything smelled like burning at once. A wall of heat lifted her off the ground and tossed her across the deck of the ship.

CHAPTER 8

Joe blinked away the spots filling his vision and tried to think.

The deck was hard and hot on his back. His ears were ringing. His head hurt. All he could see was the sky, filled with clouds of smoke and dotted with the black shapes of oncoming planes.

Slowly, he sat up and took in the scene around him.

The battleship across from the *West Virginia* had exploded, like someone had punched a hole through its middle. Flames jetted up into the sky out of its gutted belly, sending a column of pitch-black smoke into the air. Slowly, with the sea frothing around it, the back end of the ruined ship began leaning into the water.

Something landed on the deck next to Joe, making him start. It was a clipboard, the edge still on fire. The head of the paper clipped to it read: USS *Arizona*—Morning Assignments. Then the fire blackened it into a piece of fluttering ash.

All around Joe, sailors were climbing to their feet, some looking glassy-eyed and dazed, others scrambling in panic. But Joe was frozen in horror, watching the *Arizona*'s tail sink deeper and deeper into the ocean. Weren't these ships meant to be unsinkable? What sort of bomb could destroy a battleship like that?

Who was bombing them? What was happening?

All Joe knew was that everything had gone horribly, unbelievably wrong. His face, nostrils, eyes, every part of him stung and burned. He remembered his grandmother's Bible stories, about the world being plunged into a lake of fire and brimstone. This must be what it was like—the end of the world.

Out of nowhere, Skipper appeared before him. She was barking her head off and nuzzling Joe's face. It broke Joe out of his stunned gaze, and he threw his arms around Skipper's neck and shook with fear.

"Oh, Skipper," he cried, his body shaking against hers. "What's going on? Who's attacking us, girl? How did this happen?"

Skipper pulled away from him and barked, moving her head from Joe to the ship and back again. Joe felt grit biting his arm as a line of machine gun fire cracked against the deck to his left.

Skipper was right—he had to get inside the ship, out of the line of fire.

Panic kicked in, and Joe jumped to his feet and ran blindly, Skipper at his side. Around him, sailors were trying to get to their battle stations while the planes overheard kept firing on the decks of the battleships. Joe caught quick glimpses of some sailors being blown off their feet or knocked into the water by the gunfire. He tried not to think about what had just happened to them. He tried to remember where the entrance was that they'd used to get on the deck of the ship.

Suddenly, a terrible crunching noise rang out above him. Joe looked up to see one of the towers of the *West Virginia* smashed inward by a heavy black shape—a bomb. Not detonated but taller than he was, and probably twice as heavy.

With a groan, a huge chunk of the turret split off around the bomb. Joe was frozen in terror, only able to watch as it came falling toward him—

WHACK! Skipper threw her whole body into Joe's butt, knocking him forward just in time. Behind them, the hunk of tower crashed to the deck with a massive crunch. Bits of glass, wood, and metal scattered all around them.

Joe sat up, gasping, barely able to breathe. His heart pounded and sweat poured down his face. He stared at the settling pile of wreckage and thought about how if it hadn't been for Skipper, he would be under that pile of metal and glass right now, his body broken into a million pieces.

"Thanks, girl," he said, and climbed to his feet.

"HEY, JOE!"

Who was calling him? Joe followed the voice and saw Danny leaning out of a doorway that led into the ship. He waved for Joe while a bunch of other sailors yelled and tried to snatch the door out of his hand.

"Get over here!" screamed Danny. "I need to get you inside before we take serious damage!"

Joe leaped to his feet and ran toward the door. He was just about to step into the hatch when something in the distance caught his eye.

Toward the front of the ship, a broad figure sat behind one of the *West Virginia*'s .50 caliber machine guns, empty shells the size of cucumbers tumbling to the deck next to it. In quick bursts, he fired into the air, his body heaving with the kick of the gun. But it was the shape of his frame and the way he pumped his fist when one of the planes overhead exploded in flames that sent a flash of recognition through Joe's mind.

It was Pop!

Joe couldn't believe his eyes, and he felt his breath hitch in his throat. Pop, who the navy said could never be anything other than a cook, shooting down enemy planes with a gun he'd never used before!

Joe watched his father's body shake as his machine gun lit up with fireballs and spat shells from its sides. Another plane disappeared in a smoky explosion.

"Pop!" he screamed. "Pop, it's me!"

"He can't hear you over the guns!" screamed Danny. He grabbed ahold of Joe's arm. "Inside, now!"

"We can't leave him out here!" yelled Joe. "What if something happens? We can't—"

Just then, Skipper turned to the side of the ship and started her panicked barking again. This time Joe recognized it for what it was—her warning bark—and looked to where she faced. Off in the ocean at their side, a huge shape was making the water ripple in a line—heading right for them!

"Look!" shouted Joe, pointing.

"What the— Oh no," said Danny. "Torpedo! Torpedo off the port side! Prepare for impact—"

The deck under Joe kicked with a horrible rumble as the shape beneath the water hit the bow alongside them.

Joe was bounced into the air and dropped onto his back. White flashed across his vision, and then he felt the whole world lurch forward, tossing him toward the port railing of the battleship.

Before he could catch himself, Joe was sliding down the deck toward the edge. He scrambled at the deck with his fingernails and the heels of his shoes, but it was no use—he was going down!

The railing collided with Joe's stomach, knocking the wind out of him. For a brief moment, he thought of Mama and Pop, of Baby Kathy, of how sorry he was to have snuck on here and gotten mixed up in all of this. Then he lurched over the edge—

And froze in midair!

Joe stared down at the churning water below him, sloshing hard against the side of the *West Virginia*. He could see flaming slicks of oil moving up and down along the surface and sailors swimming for shore.

Why wasn't he falling toward them? How was he still alive?

He heard a growl and the scrape of nails and felt a tug at the back of his pants.

Skipper! Joe looked over his shoulder. Skipper had the back of his belt in her mouth and was leaning all the way back on her legs to pull Joe back up on the railing!

Joe reached back, felt for the railing, and grabbed it. He pulled himself back on the sloping deck and threw his arms around Skipper.

"Thank you, girl!" he cried. "You saved my life! Again!"

The ground kicked and rumbled beneath them, making Joe jump and Skipper whine.

"There'll be time to thank her later!" screamed Danny from the door. "We're getting torpedoed, kid! Get in here!"

Joe looked again for Pop. He thought he could just make him out through the smoke, collapsed but climbing to his feet, but he wasn't sure. What had happened to Pop when that torpedo hit? Had he been thrown over the edge without a Skipper to save him?

"JOE!"

Joe fought back tears. There was no time. More than anything, Pop would want him to be okay. He had to go.

Joe scrambled up the tilted deck and grabbed Danny's hand, Skipper hot on his heels. Once the sailors had pulled Joe and Skipper into the ship, Danny yanked the door shut.

Just as he did, two more kicks hit the *West Virginia*, sending them all reeling around the passageway of the battleship.

A deep groan echoed through the ship around them as the hallway leaned even deeper to the port side. All of the sailors around Joe shared wide-eyed glances, their faces slick with sweat. Among them, Joe saw Seaman Norman, shaking like a leaf and clutching the collar of his uniform.

"They're going to sink us!" shouted Norman. "They're going to sink us just like they sank the *Arizona*!"

"No, they won't," said Danny. To Joe, he looked as pale and sweaty as any of the other sailors, but there was a wild gleam in his eye that none of the others had. "Not if we can help it."

CHAPTER 9

SUNDAY, DECEMBER 7, 1941
8:11 A.M.

Danny led them down the corridor and into a room lined with three rows of bunk beds. When they got to his bed, he pulled a bag out from under it and produced a rolled-up tube of paper. He spread it out along the bed, and Joe saw a blueprint of the USS *West Virginia*, its many decks and passageways carefully labeled.

"We're taking water on our port side, right?" said Danny, pointing to one side of the ship diagram. "If we don't stop the water flow, the ship will take on too much water and capsize. We need to stop the flow on the port side by sealing all the waterproof hatches and doors. Then we have to even out the amount of water on the ship by using the counterflooding pumps on the other side to let water in."

"Let water in?" cried Norman. "You'll sink this thing!"

"If we don't, the *Wee Vee* will flip over," snapped Danny. "Don't you know what capsize means? The entire thing'll go butt-up, and everyone on deck will be pulled down with it. We can't let that happen." A murmur moved through the crowd, and Danny cursed and looked at his watch.

"I say we abandon ship," said one of the other sailors.

"If you want to leave, leave," snapped Danny. "But we don't have time to make this a discussion. We have maybe fifteen minutes—"

Another kick and rumble. The ship jumped and rocked under them. Personal items—boots, tin cups, bundles of letters—came spilling to the floor and sliding to the port-side wall.

"Or maybe only ten minutes," said Danny, a little breathless. "Are you with me or not?"

The men looked at each other, then nodded and called out that they were. Danny scanned them, and then his eyes fell on Joe.

"Joe, you with me?" he said. "We need all the help we can get."

Joe blinked and breathed hard. He felt swelling in his throat, stinging in his eyes. The last thing he wanted to do was cry in front of these men, but he couldn't control himself.

He was so scared. He just wanted to be home in bed, or in the kitchen watching Mama put the icing on Pop's cake, bouncing Baby Kathy on his knee.

"I'm not a sailor," he croaked out.

Danny knelt down in front of him and put a hand on his shoulder. The quiver of Danny's lip and the pale, sunken color of his face told Joe that Danny was scared too.

"I don't need sailors right now," said Danny. "I need heroes."

The words pushed Joe's fear back down into his stomach and made his heart swell. He thought of Pop, shooting down planes on the deck of a ship. He thought of Skipper, risking her life to

pull Joe out of the fire twice in five minutes.

If they could be brave, then so could he.

"I'm in," said Joe.

Danny smiled. "Great. Skipper, you up for it?"

Skipper barked. Joe and the other sailors laughed, maybe a little nervously.

"All right, boys," said Danny. "We go down two levels. Then you, you, and you, head port side and seal every hatch and door along the way. We can't let the water get any farther in. You, you, and you"—Danny pointed at Joe—"come starboard and help me operate the pumps. If the ship starts to go down, you all get up top and jump for it. Ready?"

"Ready!" yelled the men, Joe included.

"Let's save this ship," said Danny.

They bolted into the ship, Danny leading the way with his blueprint in his hands. Lights overhead flickered wildly. They jogged down narrow corridors, some filled with smoke, others sparking from light sockets and split panels. As they ran, other sailors came out of their rooms and joined the crew, getting filled in on the plan as they ran.

Joe put his head down and kept one hand on

Skipper. He was still terrified, of course. It was scary—the smoke, the fire, the panicked sailors. But being scared wasn't a good enough reason not to help.

They trundled down two flights of stairs, and Joe felt his feet slap into ankle-deep water. Even though it was the warm Hawaiian Pacific, his feet felt ice cold as it soaked into his shoes. Danny wiped sweat from his eyes as he studied the blueprint, and then he began pointing.

"Port-side team, you're going that way," he said, pointing. "Seal all waterproof hatches, as many as you can. Starboard team, this way to the pumps. Let's move it!"

Danny grabbed Joe's shoulder and pulled him through a doorway into another compartment.

Joe felt his hand leave Skipper's coat. He turned just in time to see her looking up at him— before Norman yanked the door shut.

"NO!" Joe screamed, and tried to run back, but Danny was pulling him along.

Skipper was gone!

CHAPTER 10

Skipper barked at the door, but no one answered on the other side. She growled and looked to the other masters to give her a hand, but they were already running off into the ship, splashing through the water.

Joe was gone! She'd lost her pup! What could she do? How would he survive without her?

Skipper knew that Joe was a good pup. He was strong and kind and smart enough to put her in the straw box to get her on board. But he was still a pup. Even the toughest ones needed to be looked after.

Now Joe was gone, leaving her surrounded by booming sounds and burning smells. It wasn't right. She couldn't just leave him.

What could she do? She didn't even know where she was, and everything was strange and unfamiliar. The ground was shifting under her, shaking and leaning to one side. There was water where there wasn't supposed to be, and it was rising quickly. Somewhere in the distance, she could hear it rushing into the ship, moving closer.

Skipper whined. She felt angry, but she also felt helpless. It made her want to run away, like she'd always done. Like she should have done the minute she noticed Joe . . .

No. Skipper put her head down and turned her growl into a bark of determination. She'd been strong enough to survive on the beaches and in the alleyways. And she'd been smart enough to find Joe, the one human who'd been really kind to her.

She would find a way back to him. There was always a way.

She ran through the halls of the ship. She did

her best to block out the sounds and smells that weren't important right now—smoke and seawater, clanging metal and whooping alarms—and tried to catch a hint of Joe or Danny. She knew if she could just get a whiff of them on the air, or could hear their voices somewhere in the distance, she could follow them. She was smart like that, able to catch a little sound or smell and follow its trail to whatever she wanted.

She'd find him, she just had to work at it.

She held up her nose, sniffed the air . . .

There! On a gust of wind, she caught it—Joe's smell, straight ahead!

She charged in the direction of the smell, but a human cry made her stop in her tracks. Through a doorway, she could see one of the humans now, not still a pup but not yet a master. He was trapped under a fallen piece of pipe and couldn't get free . . . and the water was rising around him.

Skipper paused. If she helped this human, she might not find Joe.

But if it were Joe under that pipe, and another dog didn't help him, she'd hate that dog forever. She'd find him down under the docks and bite him. Each of these pups, even the ones that were almost masters, was another dog's Joe.

Skipper darted into the room and quickly saw the problem—the human's bottom coverings were caught. It didn't help that he was panicking, yelling and thrashing and waving his arms at her. She barked at him to be quiet, then ducked her head down under the water and ripped at his coverings with her teeth. Instantly the human was free, and he scrambled to his feet and ran out of the room without so much as a "good girl" to Skipper.

In the hallway, there was just a shred of Joe smell left in the air, and she focused on it. She followed it up one staircase, then another, then another, until she was out in the open again. All around her was noise and burning, screams and flying machine roars, but Skipper stayed focused, letting Joe's smell guide her around the side of the ship. It went past the door and up some stairs into one of the towers. Could Joe have gone so far up?

At the top of the tower, Skipper stopped. It wasn't Joe there, it was Joe's father!

Joe's father stood with the man in the shiny

coat, holding him up with a big arm looped under his shoulders. The man in the shiny coat was talking in a calm voice, but he was doing a poor job of hiding that he was hurt. Even if Skipper couldn't smell the blood on him or hear his slowed-down heartbeat, she could see the dark patches on his coat.

The man in the shiny coat caught sight of her and smiled. Then he looked to Joe's father and said something. It was a lot of human talk, but Skipper understood two words: "Skipper" and "Joe."

Joe's father looked down at her, his eyes wide. Skipper saw how strong he was, but she could also smell his fear and hear his heart pounding. To try to put him at ease, she sat up straight and gave him a single bark.

Joe's father seemed hesitant, unsure what to make of her. Then he reached out and patted her head. Good, she'd won him over.

Now back to business! Skipper barked at Joe's father and swung her head and shoulders toward the door. They needed to get going! Joe, their pup, was out there in the noise and burning, along with a lot of other pups and masters who needed their help!

The man in the shiny coat slapped Joe's father on the arm and said something to him. Joe's father slowly lowered him into a chair and spoke to him in a soft voice. The man in the shiny coat pointed toward the door, said a bunch of human words, and then, "Joe!"

Finally, someone who gets it! barked Skipper.

Joe's father nodded and turned back to Skipper. She barked one more time to keep his attention— these humans could get so easily distracted, even the masters—and then ran out the door and down the stairs of the tower. Then they were on the deck, Skipper leading the way to the opening she'd come out of, retracing the smells and sounds that she'd passed.

She found the hatch—but it was blocked by a big piece of ship. And there was a human under it!

Skipper skidded to a halt, unsure what to do. Even if they could find another hatch, she didn't want to leave this master here hurt. She looked up at Joe's father, wondering what his plan was.

Joe's father looked back at Skipper. Then he put his fingers in his mouth, and—

FWEET!

Whoa! Skipper had never heard a whistle like *that* before! It made her heart race and her head rush. It was like she instantly knew what to do!

Joe's father lifted the big piece of ship. He strained and grunted, but he finally got it up high enough that Skipper could fit under it. She grabbed the hurt human by the leather strap around his waist and dragged him out of the way of the piece of ship. Then Joe's father put down the ship piece, knelt down, picked up the human, and went into the hatch.

Inside the ship, Joe's father put down the human and turned back to Skipper. He smiled down at her, and Skipper felt the same kindness and strength in him that she'd felt in Joe. They worked together perfectly. He was a good master, and she was a smart girl.

The ship shook under them, and Joe's father's smile went away as he steadied himself. He put his fingers in his mouth and whistled again, and Skipper barked in agreement.

Skipper led him down the corridor, deeper into the ship. They had other masters and pups to save, including Joe. But maybe—just maybe—they had a chance of doing it, so long as they did it together.

CHAPTER 11

"**N**o!" cried Joe as Danny pulled him away. His feet splashed in the water on the floor as he tried to get back to the door, but it was no use.

"We've got to get to those pumps, Joe," said Danny. "She'll be fine on her own. There's no time to waste."

"Get off of me!" yelled Joe. He turned his anger on Danny and began swatting at the hand that held onto his shirt and dragged him away from Skipper. "We can't just leave her! She needs me!"

Danny held Joe steady and looked into his eyes. "Look, Joe, Skipper is a smart dog, right?" he said. "She lived on the street for years. She'll be fine on her own, like she was before you found her. And if this ship capsizes, she's in just as much trouble as we are."

Through the fear and anger, Joe heard the reason behind Danny's words. Skipper was tough—she could make it on her own.

Maybe, Joe thought, he wasn't scared of her being alone, but of having to go it alone himself. He had to prove that he could be brave—for Pop, for Skipper, but most of all for himself. He clamped his mouth shut and ran with Danny and the rest of the crew.

Making their way to the valves was especially difficult with the way the ship was leaning and the water that welled up around their ankles. Pretty soon, Joe's ankles and calves burned with the effort of a steady uphill climb.

All around them, Joe heard the muffled sounds of battle through the walls: the chug of machine gun fire, the whoop of the air-raid siren, the occasional scream. Behind all of this was the rush of water and the loud, metallic groaning of the *West Virginia*.

Joe wondered what the attack meant. Up until now, the war had been something scary outside America. Pop talked about getting into the war, but Mama had mentioned that she heard news-casters on the radio saying it would never happen. Hitler and his allies in Italy and Japan would never think to attack America or any of its terri-tories. What was going to happen now? Did this mean they were at war?

They turned a corner and nearly ran into an officer making his way down the corridor. When the man turned around, Joe saw that it was Lieu-tenant Commander Harper, the cigar-chewing officer who had led them to Captain Bennion!

Harper was propping himself up against an iron hold in the wall. His face was pale and beaded with sweat. Joe noticed the dark-red stain on the right shoulder of his uniform and could see that he was struggling to stay standing. He must have gotten injured in the attack.

"Commander Harper," said Danny, going to

the man's side and putting an arm under him to help steady him.

"Cunningham?" said Harper, looking at them in disbelief. "Dean? What the blue blazes are you doing here? All of you boys need to get off this ship now. We could capsize at any moment."

"We're going to use the counterflooding valves to keep her upright," said Danny. The men with them murmured agreement.

Harper shook his head. "I'm heading there now. I'll take care of that. You boys go."

"With all due respect, sir," said Joe, "you're in no shape to go it alone. Let us help you."

"Not a chance, Dean," said Harper. "This is too dangerous for a little kid like you."

"Yeah, what else is new?" said Joe. The other men laughed, and Harper cracked a grin.

"All right," said Harper, nodding. "Then let's go, boys. Up ahead. Get to the valves, and I'll instruct you from there." They kept moving, with Joe leading the way and Danny helping Harper along as the older officer shouted directions.

Finally they reached the counterflooding

valves, a series of large metal wheels set into a wall made entirely of twisting and curling pipes. There were five in all, and the team of men split up so there were two men on each valve, with Joe and Danny next to each other on the last one.

"On three, you all turn the switches, which will open the sea cocks and let in water," barked Harper. "Turn them as far as you can, until they won't turn any farther. Once they're open, you'll hear water coming in, which means the compartments are flooding."

"Then what?" asked Norman.

"Then you run like your life depends on it, son," said Harper. "Because pretty soon this compartment's going to be flooded too. As long as you get going the minute we're done, you should be able to make it out of here."

The sailors were all silent. Even with the noise of battle around them, the counterflooding compartment felt like a church, huge and solemn.

"Ready?" asked Harper.

"Ready!" cried the men.

"Joe." Joe looked up to see Danny. He stared straight ahead, as though he were looking past the valves to the water outside. "Whatever happens, you stick with me. Don't leave my side. Do everything I do. If you can't see me, I can't see you. Got it?"

"What if I lose sight of you?" asked Joe.

Danny exhaled hard. "Then you run, Joe," he said. "Don't wait for me or search for me. You run as fast as you can, and you get off this ship." The corners of Danny's mouth twitched, and he blinked hard and fast. "And you tell Mills to be good for Mom and Dad. You tell her that I love her, and that I always will."

The last words made Joe sick to his stomach. "Danny . . . ," he said.

"And . . . TURN!" yelled Commander Harper.

There was no time to say anything else. Joe gritted his teeth and put every muscle in his body into turning the big wheel. At first it resisted, and then with a shriek of metal it began moving. And soon it was spinning so fast that the metal spokes in the wheel became a blur in Joe's eyes.

Just like that, the wheel came to a stop with a *CHUNK* noise. Somewhere deep in the ship around them, Joe heard the sound of rushing

water. For a split second, he smiled, happy they'd managed to counterflood the ship and keep it from capsizing—

And then he remembered Harper's words, and he felt a jolt like an electric shock rushing through his legs

"Now MOVE!" yelled Commander Harper. Joe and Danny turned and ran, feeling the older officer's hand slap their backs as the water began to pour in around them.

CHAPTER 12

SUNDAY, DECEMBER 7, 1941
8:24 A.M.

They did as they were told: they ran like their lives depended on it.

Because they did. The rush of water joined the sounds of the battle. The flood was coming.

The crew sprinted down the corridor. One by one, the other sailors in their group broke off and sealed the waterproof hatches to lock the flooded areas.

Joe's feet pounded the metal floor of the *West Virginia*'s corridors. The passageways and hatches began to blur together in his vision as he ran from the oncoming water.

Behind him, Commander Harper still shouted instructions while draped over Danny's shoulder, trying to keep up, but Joe couldn't really hear them over the blood pounding in his ears. He felt like if he looked back even for a second, the water would be there, a big wave with teeth of foam ready to chomp down on him and swallow him forever.

All that mattered was survival.

"There, up ahead!" yelled Harper.

Joe's eyes zeroed in on the end of the corridor. There was a set of steep metal stairs leading up to a final doorway in the wall. There it was, their end in sight.

Joe felt an extra spring in his step—they would make it!

He took the steps two at a time and then helped Commander Harper up the stairs along with Danny. Once they were through the doorway, Joe put his shoulder into the door and pushed—

A cry rang out from behind the door.

Joe froze, the hair on the back of his neck standing up. That voice . . .

He pulled the door open and looked inside.

Halfway down the passageway, Seaman Norman lay on the floor, clutching his ankle. His face was creased in a grimace of pain, and he slammed his fist into the floor while crying out. He tried to climb to his feet, but he quickly stumbled and collapsed with another shout.

"Joe, close the hatch!" shouted Danny.

Joe felt the metal of the door under his hand, cool and solid. He thought of Norman calling him "boy" and making that crack about how his father would never be anything but a cook.

It would be so easy to shove the door closed.

Too easy, thought Joe.

"Joe, no!" screamed Danny, but Joe was already through the hatch and halfway down the stairs by then. He sprinted as hard as he could toward Norman and skidded to a halt at the sailor's side.

"Come on!" yelled Joe. He knelt, put his shoulder under Norman's arm, and hefted the sailor to his feet.

"Kid, I'm done for!" shouted Norman over the rush of water. "Save yourself!"

"Not a chance," said Joe. He knew the right

thing to do, and he'd do it or die trying.

Together, they hobbled toward the staircase. At the top, Danny was calling for them to hurry, waving them on. Every step made Norman wince and grunt in pain, but he was making good progress, moving with Joe as fast as he could.

Joe was exhausted, but he forced himself to keep going. They were almost there. Just a little farther.

Then he heard a roar from behind them. In the doorway, Danny's eyes grew wide.

Joe glanced over his shoulder and saw the water coming. It crashed around a corner, bounced off the wall, and rushed toward them in a foamy blast of dark blue. And it was moving fast, coming at them far quicker than Joe and Norman could hop.

Joe saw the oncoming wave as a dark foamy fist, about to punch them in the back and knock them out forever.

Then he remembered Kai's instructions during their first surfing lesson. *You just gotta roll with the waves*, Kai had said. *Sometimes, the water is going to come at you hard and quick, and you won't know what to do. Then you just gotta ride it. The wave's going to move whether you want it to or not—you gotta decide if you're with it or against it.*

He'd never fully understood what that meant before, but he did now.

There was no fighting against this column of water. He'd just have to ride it.

"Okay, Norman," shouted Joe. "When that water hits us, it's going to try to sweep our legs out from under us. Instead, we're going to fall forward and ride it with our bodies. Just let it push you into the stairs and then get up them as quickly as possible."

"Are you nuts?" shrieked Norman. "It'll crush us in an instant!"

Joe felt droplets of water and mist prickle the back of his neck. There was no time to reassure him. "Ready?" he shouted.

"Wait!" said Norman.

Joe glanced back. The water would hit them in three—two—one—

"Now!" shouted Joe.

Just as the column of water smashed into them, Joe and Norman leaned forward and let it rush up around them. Sure enough, the water swept them up on their bellies and fired them down the passageway toward the stairs.

Joe didn't realize how fast they were shooting forward until he slammed into the stairwell. His forearms and knees clanged hard against the metal stairs, and the water hammered at his back. But he held onto Norman's arm for dear life, knowing that one slip might sweep the injured sailor away into the slowly filling passageway.

Thankfully, he quickly felt Danny's hand grabbing his shirt, and he managed to pull himself and Norman up the staircase to help Danny drag them up out of the water.

Joe and Norman fell into the corridor, dripping and gasping, while Danny and Commander Harper pushed the door against the rising flood. For a second, foamy jets of water sprayed out from the sides of the door—and then it shut with a thud. Danny and Commander Harper collapsed with their backs against it, breathing heavily.

"Well done, Sailors," said Harper between breaths. "We just might've saved this old girl from capsizing."

"Yeah." Danny panted. "Now let's just hope we can make it out alive."

Joe looked over at Norman, saw him gritting his teeth. "How bad is your ankle?" he asked.

"Hurts more than anything I've ever felt," said Norman. "Other than that, it's fine." He glanced over at Joe, and the anger and pain behind his eyes softened a little. "You saved my life, kid. I owe you one."

"You would've done the same for me," said Joe.

Norman nodded slowly, his mouth a hard, straight line. "Yeah. Yeah, I would have. Hey, where'd your dog go?"

Joe felt hurt wash over him in a wave. He'd been so caught up in counterflooding the ship that he'd forgotten about Skipper. For all he knew, she could be hurt or dead. He nodded and tried to keep his cool, but he felt his throat go tender and his eyes sting.

"Hey, kid, it'll be okay," said Norman, obviously seeing how upset Joe was. "I'm sorry I even brought it up. You'll find her. I know you will. Tough kid like you? No question."

"I just hope she's all right," said Joe.

"She seemed like a smart cookie," said Norman. He put a hand on Joe's shoulder. "Something tells me she's somewhere playing it safe."

CHAPTER 13

SUNDAY, DECEMBER 7, 1941
8:34 A.M.

Through the doorway was fire, raging with heat and billowing dirty-smelling smoke. In the corner was another pup, about Danny's age, huddled and yelling as the flames closed in.

Joe's father whistled and pointed, and Skipper followed his finger to a bundle of cloth on a shelf across the room. Just as before, it was as though she and Joe's father were one, understanding each other perfectly.

Skipper didn't even hesitate—she backed up, ran forward, and leaped over the flames to the shelf. She felt one or two of her hairs get singed, but she wasn't going to whimper about a little burned-up fur. Not when she had a job to do.

Skipper grabbed the bundle of cloth in her mouth and jumped back out of the compartment. Joe's father took it and unrolled it to reveal a heavy blanket. He whipped it into the air and let it fall over the flames—and just like that, they went out! The scared human pup got up and ran over the blanket, out of the hatch, and down the corridor.

Joe's father turned to Skipper, petted her face, and said, "Good girl."

Skipper had never wanted to run away less in her life. For the first time, she felt like she was doing what she needed to do: saving these humans. She and Joe's father had already braved water, fire, and those sparking black ropes that sent buzzing pain through the water. It had been tough, but they'd saved so many human pups that she'd lost count. It was as though she and Joe's father were speaking the same language; she would follow his whistling and pointing when he knew what to do, and he would follow her lead when she heard

shouting or crying down in the corridors of the ship.

But it hadn't all been easy. They'd been singed and shocked, slammed into walls by the rocking ship, and doused with water that reeked of fuel. Some of the pups and masters they'd found had been badly hurt, while others . . .

She couldn't think about it. She knew that the minute that she or Joe's father stopped to consider how scary everything around them was, they would be overwhelmed with the fear. They might run away.

Skipper turned to Joe's father and saw that he was doing exactly that. Joe's father planted his back against a wall, put his face to his hands, and slid down until he was sitting on the floor. Skipper barked, trying to keep his energy up. She'd heard his heart pounding away since they'd started saving humans together, and she knew he was probably becoming tired and scared.

It wasn't his fault, Skipper knew. These humans were strong and smart in some ways but weak in others. Maybe it was because they were always throwing out the best parts of their food, like the gizzards and fat. But she was running on pure excitement, and she knew that the longer they stood still, the greater the chance that both of them would lose that strength too early and not having enough energy to continue. They'd get tired and sloppy, which would only be more dangerous for them.

Besides, she could hear more noises nearby—more crashing, fire crackling, loud swishing in the water around them. And behind all of it, Skipper could hear more sounds, the kinds humans couldn't pick up on. There were crackling words in a different human language than she was used to. There were pulsing beeps that seemed to sweep out through the air around them, and steady clicks in patterns that she thought sounded like someone talking.

Whatever was happening, she knew it wasn't over. The flying machines and giant metal fish attacking them weren't done. They needed to keep moving.

Skipper saw the glazed look in Joe's father's eye and the way his lips shook as he breathed. Now, after they'd saved so many human pups, she wanted to protect him, to save him from his own thoughts and feelings.

Skipper remembered Joe clutching her as the attack had broken out. She walked to Joe's father's side, nuzzled his face, and put her head down against his chest. Joe's father wrapped his arms around her neck and buried his face in her fur. His body shook, and he breathed heavily. Skipper stood still and let him clutch her. She had felt this sorrow before when her old master had left her, and she had howled in her fear. She knew Joe's father was just howling in his human way.

Once he'd calmed down a bit, Skipper backed up and barked at him while wheeling her head down the corridor. They had more work to do. Joe was somewhere in this ship. They needed to find him.

Joe's father stared at her blankly, and for a moment Skipper wondered if he was totally broken . . . but then his brow set and he climbed to his feet. His heart beat fast and strong, and the smell of fear sweat and sadness disappeared. He'd had his moment to rest and deal with his feelings, and he could now return to the task at hand.

Joe's father put his fingers in his mouth and whistled, and they were off again.

As they continued into the ship, Skipper heard more voices. She barked for Joe's father and led him to a door from which she could hear pounding fists and panicked screams. She barked louder and nodded at the door.

Joe's father put his ear to the door, then tried to pull it open—but it wouldn't budge. He gripped the handle, put his foot up on the wall next to the door, and pulled as hard as he could. Skipper watched every muscle on Joe's father's body tighten and strain. His neck corded, his eyes clenched shut, and—

BANG! The door flew open, and Joe's father stumbled back. Water spilled out of the compartment as five soaking-wet humans came stumbling out, panicked and screaming their thanks. Two of them held up a third, who had a stream of blood coming from a wound in his head.

Joe's father spoke to them. He turned to Skipper, whistled, and said three words Skipper understood: "Skipper! Out! Go!"

Skipper didn't need to be told twice: she had

to find the outside of the ship and get the hurt human to safety. She just hoped everything would be safer outside than it was in here. She could still hear flying machines buzzing away up there, and she could smell fuel and burning all around them.

She guided them through corridors and up staircases, dancing impatiently as they took their time loading the injured human up the stairs. Joe's father was the human alpha, his orders followed by the others, but Skipper was in the lead!

They reached a passageway down which Skipper could smell and hear the outside from a distant opening—but Skipper stopped so fast that her nails scratched along the floor. Down the hall, she could see a broken tube shooting white smoke, which she knew was actually water—*steam*, the humans called it, water so hot it was smoke. From here, Skipper could feel the heat from it, and she knew the poor humans' skin wouldn't be able to take it.

Skipper thought fast. They could try to find another exit, but that could take a while, and the injured human was losing blood fast. But she could hear the steam shooting out of the pipe, and her ears followed the sound back toward the door. Through the cloud, she could make out one of those wheels on the wall like the ones these humans used to open doors.

Skipper lowered her head and ran. Joe's father called out after her. She was scared, but she knew she needed to act fast. She couldn't have them following her into the heat.

She put everything she had into her legs and bounded off the ground, through the cloud of steam. It was so hot that she couldn't help but cry out, though her fur took a lot of the heat that would've burned the humans.

She followed the rushing sound to a wheel. When she jumped up and put her paws to it, it moved under her. Listening closely for the sound of moving metal in the pipes, Skipper jumped up and put one paw over the other through the spokes of the wheel. It turned, turned . . . and then stopped.

Just like that, the steam stopped spewing from the pipe! Skipper barked to the humans, and they came forward. Joe's father smiled down at her and laughed, ruffling the fur on her head. Skipper

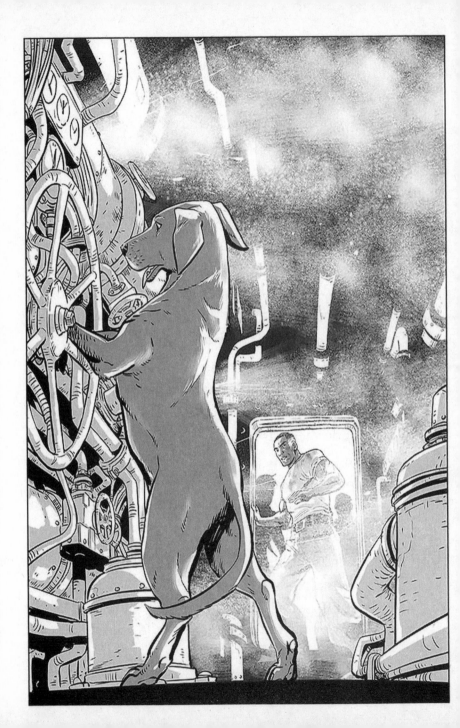

looked up at him, feeling warmth in her heart. She'd done right by Joe and his father. She was a good girl.

At the end of the corridor was a door to the outside. Joe's father put his ear to it, and after a moment he swung it wide and waved the other humans through. At the end he yelled for Skipper, and the two of them ran out onto the ship.

Skipper's mind reeled. The top of the ship had gone from bad to worse, covered with piles of wreckage and punched full of holes. The other ships around them were burning and jetting clouds of black smoke. There were even columns of black coming out from parts of the island, across the water! It seemed that the attack was happening everywhere, that her whole world was full of fire, anger, and noise.

Joe's father handed the humans they'd saved off to another group of masters, who ushered them into a boat. Once they were loaded on, the masters waved for Joe's father and Skipper to join. Joe's father waved to Skipper, and she took a step toward the boat—

BOOM!

Skipper's head snapped up. Overhead, one of the flying machines had exploded over the ship . . . and from its belly poured fire. But this fire was different—it moved like water, pouring down onto the ship.

Everywhere the fire landed, the ship burst into flames. Slowly, the flames cascaded down the deck—right toward them!

Before they could get on, the boat lowered itself down to the water by rope.

Joe's father turned to Skipper and screamed, "Go!"

He didn't have to tell her twice! Skipper turned and ran as hard as she could, feeling the heat growing behind her. Side by side, she and Joe's father bounded across the top of the ship, toward the edge . . . and the water that Skipper knew lay beyond it.

CHAPTER 14

SUNDAY, DECEMBER 7, 1941
8:40 A.M.

As they got to the door to the deck, Joe noticed the heat. The passageway around him was definitely warmer than the one they'd just come from. He wiped at the sweat forming on his brow with the back of his hand.

Danny leaned Commander Harper up against one wall and grabbed the door handle, but then he yanked his hands back and hissed angrily.

"You all right?" asked Joe.

"I'm fine," he said, shaking his red-palmed hands. "That thing's hot as a kettle, though.

Wonder what's going on outside."

"Might mean there's some sort of fire," said Harper. "Be careful. Here . . ."

Harper unbuttoned his shirt, leaving him in only a white undershirt with a stain of glistening red on one side. He tossed the shirt to Danny, and Danny covered his hands with it before turning the wheel and opening the door.

Instantly, black smoke blew into the passage. Flames licked the edges of the doorway. Joe's eyes teared up, and his throat stung as heat seared his face in a harsh gust of blazing air. Everyone coughed and squinted as Danny tried to wave the smoke out of their way so they could look outside.

The whole deck of the *West Virginia* was burning. Walls of uncontrollable orange flame flickered violently, making thunderous blowing noises as they raged. The world beyond the fire rippled with heat and was sometimes impossible to see between gusts of black smoke. Those sailors still on the *West Virginia* were clustering in patches of the deck untouched by the fire, climbing into rescue boats, or shimmying their way down on ropes.

"Oh no," mumbled Joe, dumbstruck. He couldn't believe what he was seeing, what he was feeling, as the smoke and fire whipped around his world. Once again, he remembered his grandmother's Bible stories from when he was small, her fantastic descriptions of the world ending in a storm of fire and brimstone.

But this was no story. There was nothing fantastic about it. The flames burned him, the air blinded him—it was too real.

"Fuel fire!" Danny coughed. "We've got to get off this ship ASAP! Come on!"

One by one they exited, crouching to try to stay below the worst of the smoke. But everywhere they turned, another wall of flame leaped out at them, and crept closer and closer to them. Joe felt panic grip his heart as he watched the sailors look around frantically, realizing that there was no way out.

No way out, except . . .

"We have to jump!" said Joe, pointing to the railing at the edge of the ship. A patch of railing close to them was untouched by the fire and provided a narrow passageway off of the burning apparatus. "We can go over the edge and into the water. It's the only way out."

"That's a drop of at least twenty feet!" shouted Norman over the roaring blaze. "We could break our necks jumping from that height. Besides, those waters are full of submarines. They could shoot us the minute we land!"

"It's that or stay here," said Danny.

"I'm with the kid," said Harper, nodding at Joe. "Let's do this."

The four of them limped their way over to the railing as fast as they could, the heat from the flames getting stronger the closer Joe got to the edge. In the distance, Joe could see the island, along with the dark wreck of the *Arizona* beneath a halo of debris on the surface of the ocean.

Cool ocean water, he thought as he squinted and put a hand to his face to block the heat. *Soothing Pacific water that'll wash all this heat away.* A few minutes ago he wanted to do everything in his power to escape the water, and now it was all he could think of! Where was a counterflooding valve when you needed it?

Joe got to the railing and looked over the edge at—

Fire!

His eyes bugged. His mouth clapped closed and open over and over.

The water was on fire! Beneath the bow of the ship, orange flames danced along the surface of the ocean, undulating up and down with the waves coming off of fallen wreckage and passing ships.

Joe gaped in panic—he didn't know what to do! Water wasn't supposed to burn! The sea was actually turning into a lake of fire that was going to swallow them whole.

"Fuel fires!" cried Norman at his side. "Must be the remaining fuel that was inside the *Arizona*!"

"Oh no," said Danny, his brave face finally falling. "This . . . this might be a problem."

"There has to be some other way out!" screamed Norman.

"Do you see another way out?" bellowed Harper, seizing Norman by his collar.

Joe took in the faces of the men around him. He saw anger, confusion, and fear. But for the first time, he understood how they felt, because he'd been through it all. He'd felt overwhelmed by all of those emotions, but he'd worked through them and had done what needed to be done, thanks to the bravery of his friends.

Now it was his turn to be the brave one.

Joe saw the world spin around him as he climbed up the rungs of the railing and stood, unsteadily, with one foot on the top. Everything was burning smoke, flashing flames, sloshing water. He felt dizzy, sweaty, unsure if this was a dream or if he was actually getting ready to do something so dangerous. Below him, the fire on the waves seemed to burn higher, as if to say, *Come on, little boy. Let's see what you're made of.*

"I'll signal for a rescue ship once I'm down there," he said.

The men behind him went silent. "Joe, wait," shouted Danny.

Joe looked down and gulped. He thought of a trip he, Kai, and Millie had taken to Waimea Bay, when they jumped off a fifteen-foot-high rock. Joe had been so scared that Kai had to give him a little nudge in the back to get him to go, and he'd landed right on his butt. Millie had said he fell off more than jumped off.

This time he wouldn't fall. This time he would jump.

He took a deep breath and launched himself forward. For a moment he was suspended in the air, with the whole world frozen around him—the fires burning on the water, the planes spiraling overhead, the island spewing smoke and flames, Danny's scream ringing out in the background—

And then everything came unstuck, and he dropped toward the lapping flames and inky water below.

CHAPTER 15

SUNDAY, DECEMBER 7, 1941
9:00 A.M.

CRASH!

All at once the world faded from around Joe, except for the gurgling sounds of water and the hiss of bubbles that came off of him. All the noise and madness vanished. He felt still and cool, floating in a calmer version of the world than the one he'd just come from.

Then he opened his eyes.

The world under the water was more chaotic than anything going on above. Huge pieces of wreckage from both battleships and airplanes sank around him in white clouds of bubbles. On the surface, the bottoms of boats cut along the water like black knives, moving toward the flailing arms and legs of sailors in the water. And up ahead, huge and black like some sort of castle of shadows, the wreck of the *Arizona* sat on the ocean floor, leaking a steady stream of ruined equipment and cloudy, toxic oil.

Oil, thought Joe, remembering the fires overhead. He knew that he had to swim past the fire if he wanted to break the surface safely. He heard loud splashes behind him and turned to see Harper and Norman crashing into the water. Danny came last, his arms at his sides, cloaked in bubbles.

Danny opened his eyes and saw Joe. He gave him a thumbs-up and began swimming toward him.

WHOOSH! A heavy green crate crashed into the water over Danny and smashed into the side of his head. For a moment, all Joe could see were bubbles. Then the crate sank beneath them, and he saw Danny floating, stunned in the water, unmoving. A cloud of red was beginning to flow out of the right side of his forehead.

"No!" screamed Joe under the water, but it just came out in a cloud of bubbles. With all his might, he pumped his arms and legs, powering forward toward Danny. He wrapped an arm around Danny's middle, hugging him tight to his chest. Then Joe moved his legs for all they were worth, trying to outswim the spread of the oil fires while keeping his knocked-out friend from sinking.

Quickly, Joe's chest ached. His limbs felt numb. He tried to keep swimming, but he was growing weak, lightheaded. He turned his eyes upward, to the blades of light coming down through the surface. He needed air.

He kicked . . . but Danny was too heavy! He reached up, but though his fingers were inches away from the surface, they didn't break.

Joe felt his shirt billow up around him as he and Danny began to sink toward the bottom. He tried to kick hard, but soon his limbs felt heavy. He watched the surface slowly begin to drift away . . .

The light on the water was blotted out by a

shadow. Two hands broke the surface and seized his outstretched fingers. The hands pulled, and the surface rushed to meet him.

The gasp of air that Joe sucked down was the sweetest thing he'd ever tasted. He heaved with breath as the two men pulled him onto the boat. He slumped onto a bench along the boat's edge and panted for dear life as the men who'd rescued him laid Danny down on the floor. By the crossed anchor insignia on their uniforms, Joe knew they'd been rescued by the coast guard. While one of the men began pumping on Danny's chest, the other began pulling Harper and Norman out of the water behind them.

Danny's skin was pale and clammy. The wound on his forehead leaked red rivulets through the water on him. Joe thought he looked dead already.

The coast guard officer pinched his nose and blew into his mouth. Then he put his hands on Danny's chest again, one, two, three—

Danny lurched, and seawater bubbled out of his mouth. The officer turned him on his side and slapped him on the back to get him to spit it all out. Joe had never been so excited to see someone throw up.

They got Harper and Norman aboard and got them stabilized; both of them looked pale as death but were conscious and speaking. Then the coast guard officer fired up the boat's motor and aimed it toward shore, with his partner standing at the front scanning the sea for more sailors to rescue.

As they drifted, Joe took in the madness around him. The *West Virginia*'s deck was burning like crazy, sending pieces of flaming ship sailing down into the water around them. The other battleships along the row were all at least partially destroyed, their decks smoking and burning.

Joe saw a line of sailors standing on a huge gray shape that he assumed was a surfaced submarine . . . until he saw the massive propeller jutting out of the water at one end.

"Is that the bottom of a ship?" he asked, almost unable to believe it.

"That's right," said Harper. "The USS *Oklahoma*, by the looks of it. It must have taken on too much water and capsized entirely."

"That's why you counterflood," croaked a distant voice.

"Danny!" said Joe, kneeling down next to his friend. Danny's eyes had finally opened. His breathing was slow, but he managed a smile. "You okay, man?"

"I'm all right," said Danny, sitting up with a groan. "Just need to get onshore and never leave again."

As they puttered over to the capsized *Oklahoma* and picked up four more sailors, Joe scanned the horizon for Pop or Skipper. There was so much wreckage floating in the splashing waves around them that it was hard to pick out one thing from another. A number of times the thing that he was almost positive was a dog turned out to be a piece of debris or a floating shirt.

"Have you heard anything about a Marcus Dean?" he asked one of the coast guard officers. "He was a mess officer from the *West Virginia*?"

"Sorry, kid, haven't heard anything," he said.

Joe's heart sank. He gulped and tried to fight

through it. "What about a dog?" he asked.

The coast guard officer squinted at him. "A dog?"

"Look!" All heads turned to Seaman Norman, who was having a fit pointing over the edge of the boat. "Over there! I heard her, honest to God! It's the same bark as before!"

One of the coast guard officers began trying to restrain Norman, but then Harper began pointing and shouting too.

Joe went to the edge of the boat and peered into the bobbing waves full of debris.

Whuff!

There! In the distance, he could make out Skipper paddling her way through the smoke and wreckage. She was dragging something with her . . . a person, someone big, by the looks of her struggling . . .

"She's got my dad!" shouted Joe. And now, after all he'd been through, tears finally poured from Joe's eyes and rushed down his face. "It's Pop! Skipper saved him!"

EPILOGUE

"Yesterday, December 7, 1941," said President Roosevelt, "a date which will live in infamy . . ."

"Joe, turn that radio off," said Mama. "The noise is tough on my nerves."

"Never get tired of it," said Pop with a laugh. He held Baby Kathy to his chest and bounced her as she cooed and giggled. "It's rare you get to hear history as it happens. Heck, if I get the Navy Cross, I'll be part of history!"

"Joe," said Mama, "the radio, please."

Joe went to the radio and turned off the rerun of President Roosevelt's war declaration. He had to agree with Mama—he'd heard the speech at least a dozen times since it had been made. He wouldn't mind a little quiet.

Joe weaved his way back to Pop's bedside. Getting around the hospital room was difficult; the place had become a maze of flowers, balloons, and cards . . . along with plenty of dog biscuits and chew toys.

In the two days since the attack, over a dozen different sailors had come forward with a story about Marcus Dean and his wonder dog. If half of what Joe had heard was true, Pop had saved countless men, but he couldn't have done it without Skipper's help. The press had picked up the story and was running piece after piece on the hero dog of Pearl Harbor. Now every grateful family, newspaper, and local business wanted to make sure Pop was furnished with flowers and decorations.

It was Pop's other heroic acts that had interested the navy. Pop had shot down fourteen Japanese planes (only now did they know it was the Empire of Japan who had attacked Pearl Harbor), and he had protected Captain Bennion through the brunt of the attack. That, plus his heroics with Skipper, had led to rumors that he would receive the Navy Cross, an award that until now had never been given to a black man. Mama said it was making him "a symbol of hope for black people everywhere." Joe just thought he was the greatest.

"Besides, we got a family of Pearl Harbor heroes here!" said Pop. "The president's talking to men like us!" He reached out one arm and pulled Joe in for a hug. Then he let his hand drop over the edge of the bed to scratch Skipper on the head. Skipper had sat diligently by Pop's side since they brought him into the hospital, breaking only to let Joe take her for walks.

"Are you going to try to get a combat position, Pop?" asked Joe. "Once you get better, of course."

"You know it," Pop said, giving him an extra squeeze on the shoulder. "Now that we're at war, I want to meet the guys who planned this attack and give them a piece of my mind."

"Not so fast, buddy," said Mama. "You've got a ways to go before the doctors declare you fit to serve, and you've got a son and a baby at home."

"I know, honey, but I can't just forget that there's a war on," said Pop. "Right, Skipper?" Skipper barked, getting a smile and another ear scratch from Marcus.

"Whatever happens, I'm just glad you're safe for now," said Mama. She leaned in and kissed him on the cheek. Joe could see that even though the idea of Pop going to war pained his mother, some of the determination and moxie floating around had rubbed off on her. Mama's home had been attacked too. She knew something needed to be done.

"Joe?" Joe looked up to see Millie at the door. On her blouse was the pin Joe had started seeing all around Oahu. It featured a rippling American flag and the words "Remember Pearl Harbor."

"Hey, Millie," he said. He was happy to see her, but his heart ached a little when he remembered why she was here. "Is Danny ready?"

"He is when you are," said Millie. "Hey, Mr. Dean, congratulations on all your recognition."

"I'm just happy we made it out alive," said Marcus. "And I owe a lot of that to our friend here. Take good care of her." Marcus put his fingers in his mouth and whistled. Skipper leaped up and put her paws on the side of the bed, and Marcus leaned over and gave her a hug around the neck. "Thank you, Skipper. Be a good girl and go with Joe."

Joe snapped a leash on Skipper's new collar—a gift from a local pet store—and he and Millie walked Skipper in the hospital hallways. They were almost at the door when a voice made Joe stop in his tracks. He crept to a nearby room door and peeked in.

"Well, they need to change their policy," said Seaman Norman to the ring of soldiers circled around him. He had his foot in a cast dangling over his bed via a sling. His own room was filled with cards and flowers, though his cards had more pin-up girls on them than Pop's did.

"What, and let colored folks serve?" asked one of the sailors.

"Darn right," said Norman. "We're all in this

together. We can't act like one group of people's any better than another."

"Aw, come on, Norman," said Mulvaney, the other sailor from the dock. "You were saying just last week that colored folks don't have what it takes to serve."

"You're right, Mulvaney," said Norman after a moment of silence. "I did say that. But I was wrong, dead wrong. Until Sunday, I didn't know what I was talking about. When I was on that ship, I learned that brave is brave, no matter what color you are or where you come from. We're not going to win this war thinking the opposite." He sighed. "Wish I'd known that. It's a cryin' shame that it took Sunday for me to learn it. But I'll never forget it."

"Tell it again, Norman," said one of the other sailors. "Tell us how it happened."

"All right, one last time," he says. "So we've just counterflooded the *Wee Vee*. I land on my foot wrong and pretty much break the damn thing. I'm hobbling down this passageway hearing the water behind me and thinking, *Welp, this is it.*

And who comes running toward me but Marcus Dean and his dog!"

What! *Marcus* Dean? Joe felt a flash of anger. He'd saved Norman, not Pop! He considered running in there and telling everyone that it had been him who'd saved Norman—

No. He exhaled his anger and turned away. Let Pop have the story. Norman probably just didn't want to admit that he'd been saved by a kid. Besides, it sounded like Norman had gotten the important part of the message. Joe was just happy to be alive and safe.

Downstairs, Danny was waiting next to his jeep. Someone had told Pop that Danny was being called a hero for leading the counterflooding charge on the *West Virginia* (even if the ship did eventually sink, despite their efforts). Up close, Joe thought he seemed a little pale and tired to be a hero—he looked almost entirely recovered, but Joe still noticed his peaked complexion and the bandage on his forehead.

"You look good!" said Joe as they approached.

"Better than I *did*, anyway." Danny laughed.

He shook Joe's hand. "Thanks for doing this, Joe. I think you're making the right choice, and I know the boys'll be grateful."

Joe nodded through his sadness. "Yeah," he said. "Skipper belongs with the navy. After what happened on Sunday, I figure you guys need a dog as smart as she is, especially if you're going to war. Just promise me you'll bring her home to visit, okay? Don't let her fall in love with some French poodle and stay in Europe."

"I'll do my darnedest." Danny laughed.

Joe knelt down in front of Skipper. She looked at him with attentive but worried eyes; Joe knew that she could tell what was going on. She whined a little and gave Joe a lick on the face.

"I wish I could've known you longer, Skipper," he said. "Thank you for saving my life, and for helping my dad. We never could've done this without you." Joe felt his eyes sting. This time he didn't try to act brave—he just let the tears flow. "I'll never forget you. And I'll see you real soon, okay?"

He threw his arms around Skipper's neck and

buried his face in her fur, smelling the salt of the sea and feeling the beating of her heart. Then he let her go and took a step back.

"Up, Skipper," said Danny, patting the bed of his jeep.

Skipper looked from Joe to Danny and back again.

"Up, Skipper," said Joe, his voice cracking. This time Skipper obeyed, and she hopped up into the back of the jeep. Danny waved goodbye to Joe and Millie, hopped in the front seat, and got the jeep grumbling to life. Then he drove off, with Skipper looking back at Joe until they were out of sight.

Joe wiped his cheeks with the back of his hand. "Sorry," he said to Millie.

"You don't need to be sorry," she said. "It's okay to feel upset. She was your friend. But I agree with Danny—this is the right thing to do."

"I'm just going to miss her a lot," said Joe. "I don't think I'll ever find another dog as great as her."

"About that," said Millie with a strange smile.

"Come with me. Kai wants to show you something."

They got on their bikes and rode through the streets of Oahu, weaving between crowds of people. Everyone was out in full force today, helping board up shops that had been hit with machine gun fire and collecting necessities like blankets and food for people whose homes had been destroyed in the attack. Memorial shrines had popped up along the main streets, and dozens of people lit candles and placed flowers in memory of their loved ones. The biggest crowds were at the recruiting office, where men and women were lined up around the block hoping to offer their help in the war effort. Almost all of them wore a pin with the slogan "Remember Pearl Harbor" on it.

Joe could tell that this was only the beginning. Sunday had left everyone feeling panicked, upset . . . and determined. They'd remember, all right.

"Look, there he is," said Millie. She pointed to a shrine in front of a storefront full of bullet holes. Kai stood there with his shoulders hunched along with several older native Hawaiian people. They all circled a pile of candles and flowers surrounding pictures of older men and women. Joe and Millie stopped and watched as Kai draped a white lei over one picture and began to walk away.

"Kai!" called Joe. They came up next to their friend. Joe had never seen him look so sad. "What's up? What were you doing?"

"It's just a memorial for the man who owned that shop," said Kai. "He passed away during the attack. My family knew him, but my parents were busy, so I came to throw a lei. It's a tradition."

"Huh," said Joe. "I didn't even think about Hawaiians having funerals."

Kai's expression darkened with anger. "Because all we do is surf, right? And dance the hula, and sell shell necklaces, and make rum drinks for stupid sailors on the beach . . ."

Then Kai broke down crying. Joe was stunned—he didn't know what had happened, and he'd never seen Kai cry before, even when he'd gotten bumped or scraped while they'd been out on their bikes.

Without thinking, he hugged his friend, and Millie hugged them both. Joe even felt himself crying a little, just a few tears. A few days ago, he would've been embarrassed to let anyone see him cry. Today, he felt like he'd earned it.

"Sorry," said Kai, pulling away from them and wiping his face with the back of his hand. "I didn't mean to get angry at you. It just seems like sometimes, with everyone saying, 'Remember Pearl Harbor,' they forget about Hawaii. Like the Hawaiians who died are less important than the soldiers."

"It's all right," said Joe. He remembered what Seaman Norman had said in the hospital. "We're all in this together."

"No matter what," said Millie.

Kai sniffed. "Thanks, guys." He gave Joe a sad smile. "Millie told me about Skipper. I'm sorry about that."

"It's okay," said Joe. "I think she'll do well with the navy. I'm just sad that I don't have a dog anymore."

Kai and Millie shared a glance and a smile. "My bike's over this way," said Kai, waving them down the street. "Follow me."

They rode into a nice suburb and down to the beach where the three of them had first met. They dropped their bikes, and Kai led them along the beach, smiling the whole time. Whenever Joe asked what was up, Millie shushed him. Finally, they reached a patch of tall grass on the edge of the beach, and Kai waved Joe forward. Joe crept up and parted the grass.

They were island puppies—three tiny dogs with patchy colors in their fur and long, pointed faces. They were wrestling, tumbling, and growling in high-pitched little voices. Joe felt his heart leap as he watched them fall all over one another.

"I saw their mom get caught by the local dog catcher yesterday and found them here," said Kai. "I figure there's one for each of us."

"Maybe you can teach them to be as smart as Skipper," said Millie.

"Maybe," said Joe, but he wasn't really paying attention. He got down on his knees, and the pups stopped playing and looked at him. He extended a hand, and one of them walked up tentatively, smelled it, and gave it a lick.

Joe thought about the past couple days, about all he'd been through and seen. He knew things were going to be different—for him, for Pop, for the entire world. But for now he could enjoy this moment, knowing that he'd done what was right, and that he was lucky for everything he had.

Nighttime. The ship lay quiet, the men inside having eaten, cleaned up, and headed to bed.

Skipper stood on the deck of the boat and felt the sea breeze move through her fur. She missed Joe, but she had to admit that she liked it here at night.

Skipper knew she wasn't supposed to be up on deck, but she'd found a way to get out of her room in the ship, a crack between two pipes. The humans would have to get used to it—she was beginning to understand that this was her new home, on the ship with Danny. If that was the case, she had to know every way in and out of her room. She'd have to memorize every smell in every corner of this boat.

After all, these humans would need protecting when they weren't ready for it. She'd have to be there whether they'd come to let her out or not.

She saw a flicker of lightning out on the ocean that made her whine. It had been an exciting few days, with meeting Joe, being on the ship during all the noise and burning, saving the human pups with Joe's father, and now here, on a boat surrounded by human pups who all seemed to like her. She wondered what else might happen soon—what other scary things and hapless humans might cross her path.

No matter what, she was ready for it. These humans were her pups, all of them, and she'd protect them with everything she had.

For a moment she caught Joe's smell on the air, and she looked over at the lights on the island. She missed him, but she knew that Joe would be okay. He had Joe's father and Joe's mother to look out for him. And anyway, he was a smart pup. Resourceful, brave, and kind.

After enjoying one last breath of night air, Skipper headed back to the door down into the

ship. She silently crept along the corridors, slipping between the pipes and into her room in the back of the kitchen. She lay down on the bed of towels the humans had given her and rested her head. She had better sleep. It was a tough time to be a dog, and tomorrow was another busy day.

BATTLE FACTS

Pearl Harbor isn't just a dramatic setting—it was one of the most important military attacks in history. It was the most deadly attack by a foreign nation on US soil, and a turning point for World War II.

Here are some handy facts to know about Pearl Harbor and how it affects this story . . .

What happened at the battle of Pearl Harbor?
At 7:55 a.m. on December 7, 1941, the Empire of Japan attacked the United States at Pearl Harbor, America's most important naval base in the Pacific, located on the island of Oahu in Hawaii Territory (Hawaii was not yet a US state at the time of the attack).

The Japanese attacked Pearl Harbor with six aircraft carriers and five submarines, and they did so without provocation or any formal declaration of war. The attack focused on multiple spots in and around Pearl Harbor, including Hickam Airfield and Wheeler Army Airfield. The most concentrated attack was on Battleship Row, a collection of eight US battleships that were moored next to Ford Island.

The attack lasted only ninety minutes, but it cost over two thousand Americans their lives. Several battleships were destroyed, most notably the USS *Arizona*, which exploded and sank, and the USS *Oklahoma*, which capsized. The next day, President Franklin Delano Roosevelt declared that America would join the war against Japan and its allies, most notably Nazi Germany.

PEARL HARBOR STATS

DATE: December 7, 1941

LOCATION: Island of Oahu, Hawaii Territory

DURATION OF ATTACK: Approximately 90 minutes

STRENGTH OF JAPANESE FORCES: 6 carriers, 2 battleships, 8 tankers, 9 destroyers, 23 submarines, 5 midget submarines, approximately 390 planes

AMERICAN SHIPS SUNK: 4 battleships, 1 harbor tug, 4 midget submarines

JAPANESE AIRCRAFT DESTROYED: 29

KILLED: 2,335 military, 68 civilians

WOUNDED: 1,143 military, 103 civilians

Night of December 6 / Morning of December 7:

Washington receives intelligence that Japan is planning a major attack. Word reaches Washington four hours before the attack on Pearl Harbor commences, but there is not enough intelligence to determine where the attack will be. By the time it reaches officials in Hawaii, the attack has already begun.

December 7, 7:35 a.m.:

Japanese commander Mitsuo Fuchida gives orders to his men, *"To ra, to ra, to ra,"* meaning that a surprise attack has been achieved.

6:45 AM   **7:35 AM**

DECEMBER 6, 1941   **DECEMBER 7, 1941**

December 7, 6:45 a.m.:

A Japanese mini-submarine is sunk off the coast of Oahu by the destroyer USS *Ward*, marking the first casualty of the attack. Admiral Husband E. Kimmel is informed of this but is hesitant to act as there have been many false reports of subs in the area.

PEARL HARBOR ATTACK

December 7, 7:55 a.m.:
Commander Logan Ramsey notices the first fighter planes dropping bombs from his post on Ford Island. Ford Island transmits the following message via telegraph: "AIR RAID ON PEARL HARBOR X THIS IS NOT A DRILL."

December 7, 8:19 a.m.:
The *Arizona* begins sinking to the bottom of the harbor.

| 7:55 AM | 8:10 AM | 8:19 AM | 9:25 AM |

December 7, 8:10 a.m.:
The USS *Arizona* is hit with an armor-piercing bomb and explodes; 1,100 men are believed to be killed instantly by the explosion.

December 7, 9:25 a.m.:
The attack ends, though for the men stationed at Pearl Harbor, the day continues for five hours of chaos and turmoil.

Q&A ABOUT THE ATTACK ON PEARL HARBOR

Q. Why was Pearl Harbor attacked?

A. The Japanese attacked Pearl Harbor as a preemptive measure to keep the navy's Pacific Fleet from interfering in maneuvers they had planned in Southeast Asia. Shortly after the bombing of Pearl Harbor, Japanese attacks were recorded in US-held countries, including Guam and the Philippines.

Of course, the attack backfired. Rather than cripple the US Navy and keep America out of the war, Pearl Harbor brought America into the war, which ended when they dropped an atomic bomb on Japan in 1945.

Q. Was Battleship Row the only site of the attack?

A. No. Japanese planes also bombed nearby Hickam Field and Wheeler Field, both US airfields, to cripple any sort of air response by American personnel. Several places in Oahu were also shot and destroyed, though some of this damage was caused by friendly fire from Americans who didn't know where the attack was coming from.

Q. What led up to the attack?
A. By December 1941, the war in Europe and Asia had reached a critical peak. Adolf Hitler, ruler of Germany and leader of the Nazi Party, had already taken over Czechoslovakia, Poland, and France. He was rounding up people he considered inferior to Germans—Jews, homosexuals, and black people, as well as other groups—and sending them to ghettos and eventually concentration camps. By 1941, the Nazis had begun bombing cities in Great Britain.

Meanwhile, the Empire of Japan, seeking more wealth and international power, had taken part in several vicious conquests in Asia. In 1940, Hitler signed a three-part pact with Italy and Japan, creating what was known as the Axis.

During this time, the United States stayed out of the war. In fact, many Americans argued that the war was none of America's business. The bombing of Pearl Harbor changed all of this, bringing the US into the war whether they wanted to or not.

Q. Were the characters in the book all actual people?

A. Some, but not all of them. Certain characters, like Captain Mervyn Bennion and Lt. Commander John Harper, were actual sailors on board the *West Virginia*. Joe, Danny, and Skipper are fictional, though Joe's father, Marcus, is based on an actual hero of Pearl Harbor named Dorie Miller.

Q. Who was Dorie Miller?

A. Doris "Dorie" Miller was an African American mess attendant on board the USS *West Virginia* during the attack. Miller manned an antiaircraft gun when its crew was disabled, and he is believed to have shot down over twenty Japanese planes. He is also credited as having gotten Captain Bennion to safety during the attack and saving several sailors who had been injured or had been thrown overboard.

For his heroics, Miller was the first African

American to be awarded the Navy Cross. More important, he helped change the navy's mind on whether or not to allow black sailors in combat positions.

Before Pearl Harbor, mess attendant or steward was about as high up that a black sailor could go in the navy. After Miller's story reached the world, and thousands of young black men began enlisting, the navy decided to change its policy. Though it remained divided by race, it allowed enlistment of all qualified personnel in 1942.

Q. Were mascot dogs really a part of the navy?
A. Absolutely! Both the United States Navy and British Royal Navy have a long history of dogs joining ships' crews. Sometimes these dogs were just pets that the sailors on board considered good luck, like Dogo, who lived on a freighter that traveled 160,000 miles between 1941 and 1942 without being harmed. Others, like Blackout, the mascot dog of a coast guard–manned Landing Craft Infantry ship, saw action on the beaches of Sicily and Normandy.

Perhaps the most famous sea dog of all time was Judy, an English pointer who was stationed aboard the HMS *Grasshopper*. The *Grasshopper* was bombed by Japanese planes, and Judy and her sailors were marooned on a desert island. Judy led them to fresh water and helped them find food on the island. When the sailors were captured by the Japanese and placed in a prisoner of war camp, Judy intervened when angry guards attempted to beat them. When the men freed the camp, Judy fended off wild animals, including tigers and crocodiles! For her bravery, Judy was awarded the Dickin Medal, considered the Navy Cross for animals.

Q. What kind of weapons were onboard the USS *West Virginia*?
A. The USS *West Virginia*'s weapons, or "armament" in military language, were extensive. The ship had eight sixteen-inch, .45 caliber Mark 1 guns located in four twin gut turrets on the fore and aft of the ship; sixteen five-inch, .51 caliber guns; four five-inch, .25 caliber guns; and two twenty-one-inch torpedo tubes.

Q. What kinds of jobs were there on a US battleship?

A. A navy battleship was like a miniature city, with over a thousand sailors living on the average ship. These sailors were generally divided into several groups, most notably seamen, who were your everyday sailors; aviators, who focused on air combat from battleships and aircraft carriers; construction workers, who worked to build and repair the equipment on board a ship; engineers, who focused on the internal workings of the ship; and mess officers or stewards, who prepared the meals and kept the ship in order. But these are only some of the ranks included in the navy at large. There were also cryptologic technicians, who focused on codes and electronic messages; chaplains, who provided spiritual support to the sailors on board a ship; and even musicians, who played in navy bands!

Q. What kind of planes did the Japanese arrive in, and what kinds of weapons did they use?

A. The Japanese used a wide variety of planes and weapons to attack Pearl Harbor. The planes that hit Battleship Row and the USS *West Virginia* were Nakajima B5N *Kate* bombers armed with 800 kg (1,760 lb.) armor-piercing bombs, and B5N bombers armed with Type 91 torpedoes. These planes were also armed with machine guns used for firing on ships as they passed.

Q. How did radio broadcasts play into the attack on Pearl Harbor?

A. As the primary form of technological communication at the time, radio played a large part in Pearl Harbor. It was said that the Japanese pilots coming to attack Pearl Harbor only knew they were nearby when they began to hear hula music over their radios.

But the most famous radio broadcast about Pearl Harbor occurred the day after the attack, when President Roosevelt gave the "Pearl Harbor speech," also known as the "infamy speech" because of its opening lines: "Yesterday, December 7, 1941, a date which will live in infamy, the United States of America was suddenly and deliberately attacked by naval and air forces of the Empire of Japan." The speech was the most listened to radio broadcast in history, with over 81 percent of Americans tuning in to listen. It also formally announced the United States as part of the growing war abroad, from which the United States had remained separate until then.

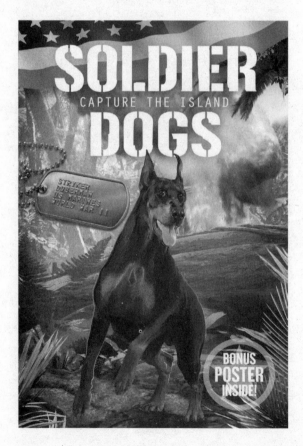

A squadron of enemy soldiers ran toward the field hospital. Bullets whined past the hiding spot where Stryker the war dog was crouching.

A mortar shell exploded nearby, digging chunks out of the earth and throwing dirt against Stryker's furry coat.

Stryker felt the urge to fight in his chest. He wanted to growl, but he'd been trained to stay quiet. His hackles raised as the enemy soldiers raced closer to him and the boy—and to the hospital behind them—but he didn't move.

He stayed with the boy called Tasi.

Tasi *hadn't* been trained. He didn't know about enemies or sneak attacks. The boy wasn't armed with a weapon—or even with teeth and claws. That's why Stryker needed to keep close.

Stryker felt his muscles tense. He'd wait here, hidden behind the fallen tree, until the enemy came near enough. Then he'd leap at them and show them what a war dog could do.

He felt Tasi trembling beside him. That was okay. Humans got scared. Even Marines got scared. Fear made humans' hearts beat faster and their eyes widen. It made their senses sharp and alert—almost as sharp and alert as a Doberman's.

Stryker was afraid that Tasi would stand and fight despite his fear. He needed the boy to run. That was the only way he'd survive. The moment that Stryker threw himself at the enemy, the boy needed to *flee*.

He needed to live.

Stryker nudged Tasi's arm, telling him to get ready to move. Tasi could scramble through the hospital behind them, past the sickbeds and the bandaged patients—if he left now.

"Don't worry, boy," Tasi whispered. "I'm right here."

Stryker nudged him again. He didn't know what those words meant, but he knew the boy wasn't getting ready to run.

"I—I'll take care of you," Tasi said, in a shaky voice.

Gunfire ripped into the other side of the tree, shredding the wood into splinters. Tasi ducked his head, his black hair short and silky.

Pain stung Stryker's muzzle. He narrowed his

eyes and gathered his rear legs to leap, tracking the enemy's position with his pointy ears. Rifles cracked and big Navy guns boomed from the US ships off-shore.

Stryker heard a scuffle and the gasp of hand-to-hand fighting. He smelled bitter smoke and sweet gasoline.

The enemy was ten strides away before Stryker let himself make a sound. He snarled at the boy telling him to run!

Tasi grabbed a branch from the ground. "W-we almost made it," he said. "We almost made it."

Stryker growled. *Get moving!*

"You and me," Tasi said, tears in his eyes. "Together till the end."

Love dogs?
You may also like...

 KATHERINE TEGEN BOOKS
An Imprint of HarperCollins Publishers

HARPER
An Imprint of HarperCollinsPublishers

HARPER FESTIVAL
An Imprint of HarperCollinsPublishers

www.harpercollinschildrens.com